TORO!
TORO!
TORO!
WILLIAM HJORTSBERG

SIMON AND SCHUSTER · NEW YORK

DESIGNED BY EVE METZ
MANUFACTURED IN THE UNITED STATES OF AMERICA

1 2 3 4 5 6 7 8 9 10

LIBRARY OF CONGRESS CATALOGING IN PUBLICATION DATA

Hjortsberg, William, 1941–
  Toro! Toro! Toro!
  I. Title.
PZ4.H677To [PS3558.J6]   813'.5'4   74-4314
ISBN 0-671-21798-4

lunes

TWO CRITICS OF THE ART sat by the window of a dank, ill-lit place and ordered cigars. Not far away, at his favorite table in the corner, the empresario Don Pepe Bacalao y Piñas was having his boots shined while he read the morning newspaper. At his side, el Chicote, a novillero badly panned in the early edition, glowered at the two critics. "Cowards," the young sword hissed. "Fairies, maricones!"

The critics laughed at these insults. They gestured with their cigars and traces of cryptic skywriting drifted above the lunch-hour crowd.

"Mariposa faggot mother-milkers," el Chicote growled.

"Patience, muchacho." Don Pepe placed a paternal hand on the young man's shoulder. "There will come another day." The empresario scanned the review for the third time, dwelling on the choicer slurs: "feeble veronicas . . . feet dancing with cowardice at every pass . . . a more graceful killing style is on display at any village carnicería." He knew it would be some time before his boy had another booking in the capital.

El Chicote scooped a handful of anchovy-stuffed olives

from a bowl on the table, catapulting them into his mouth one at a time with his thumb. His killer's eyes never left the two by the window. When the olives were gone, he went to work on the toasted almonds. Chicote had no money for lunch. The tailor's bill for his traje de luces consumed his share of yesterday's meager purse. His tight yellow satin pants had split during a tossing in the arena, spilling the fragrant yield of his fear-loosened sphincter as the crowd jeered, "Show us the color of your guts."

Don Pepe could not bring himself to look in his protégé's eyes. He stared at the poster-covered walls above the wine barrels behind the bar, mesmerized by the bold brush strokes of caping and killing. Only the illustrious names, legible as a bank statement, anchored him to reality. "Every one worth ten million pesetas," he mused, remembering the cuff links pawned this morning. The word EXTRAORDINARIO! held his gaze like the eye of a snake.

"Pues, hombre," the novillero said at last, his chair scraping on the tiles as he got to his feet.

Don Pepe nodded, glancing down at the empty olive bowl with regret. "Hasta mañana, torero," he mumbled, not looking up, avoiding the young man's haunted glance. He had enough for another brandy, but handouts were a luxury he couldn't afford.

El Chicote left the bar with a haughty swagger, spitting a chewed toothpick in the direction of the critics' table. He was ignored, as always. Don Pepe examined the boy's footprints in the sawdust; Chicote's step seemed firm and valorous on the barroom floor, quite unlike the reluctant fear-trudge his slippers had traced in the packed sand of the arena.

The castanet snap of the bootblack's rag caught the empresario's attention.

"Watch, patrón," pleaded a dark-eyed gypsy genuflecting before his gleaming boots. His filthy khaki shirt hung in tatters over a rib cage a xylophonist might have played a tune on. "Just give me a minute of your time, por favor."

Don Pepe made a gesture of confusion as the gypsy unfurled his shoeshine rag, whipping it about his emaciated body like a black, spineless muleta. "Look at this style, señor." He slipped a stick under the cloth to stiffen it and began a series of fluid naturals, his pelvis thrust professionally, bending from the waist with the grace of Ordóñez, immortalized on a wall poster above him. Next, a pase de pecho, followed by two breathtaking brazo profundos and a perfect pirandello. The astounded empresario sputtered with embarrassment, while the bootblack spun through an entire faena, his bare feet stamping in the sawdust. "Hola, toro," he grunted. "Hah, ha-ha!"

The critics applauded when the boy was done. "Quickly, give him a contract, empresario," the fat one called. "Don't let this gold mine slip through your fingers."

The gypsy stood panting, his blackened face streaked with sweat. He beckoned to a nearby waiter, "Hey, Miguelito, bring the chair with the knives and I'll show this man what I can really do."

Don Pepe lumbered to his feet, swallowing air. "Bravo, bravo," he muttered, doing his best not to look at the gypsy boy. Why me? he thought. Why do they all come to me? Without a word, he dropped a scattering of coins on the table and fled into the street.

El Chicote crossed the railroad tracks, a swordcase clamped under his arm. His shoes filled with cinders. His shirt collar was grimed with soot. A bumper crop of radishes could have been raised under his fingernails. El Chicote lacked even the admission price of the public bath. Since being evicted from his pensión, the struggling young matador slept in the metro and under bridges. There was no room service and it was hard to keep clean.

On a siding spur off the main line stood the low brick walls of the slaughterhouse, backed by loading docks and holding pens. Dust devils raced about the empty corrals. Several spotted steers stared at him through the wooden slats as he entered.

The foreman, a burly man wearing a long rubber apron and hip boots, stood hosing down the concrete floor. El Chicote waited for him to finish, nervously smoking a long lipstick-tinted butt, the prize find of the morning, while the foreman took his time, coiling the hose and double-checking to see that the water was tightly shut off. "No beef today," he said at last, crossing his bushy arms on his chest. "Only mutton."

"I've walked a long way," el Chicote answered, knowing the man considered him a tramp. "Better lambs than nothing."

"It's up to you." The foreman shrugged. "But if you make a mess like last time, I'd as soon use the hammer."

"There will be no mess. I practice the descabello today; very swift and clean." He unstrapped the leather sword-case and drew out a long-bladed estoque, marching like an acolyte in a holy procession as he followed the foreman into the gloomy depths of the building. Wedged in a narrow pen at the far end were several dozen bleating sheep.

"Take your pick and get started," the foreman said. "I got some sharpening up to do."

El Chicote entered the pen. The woolly animals bumped about his knees, their deerlike hoofs tapping on the concrete. Reaching down, he took one by the ear, glimpsing a wide fear-filled eye as he pushed the head into position.

"Hah, toro," he whispered, sighting straight down the gleaming blade. He stamped his foot once for emphasis, and was answered by a mournful *Baaa!*

Paco Machismo moved about the billiard table in the game room of his town house with the sliding grace of a caged leopard. He set his bottle of Pepsi back in the ice bucket and considered the shot from another angle. He liked the clicking sound the ivory balls made on contact: a crisp, decisive snap as pleasurable as the roaring voice of the crowd. In the arena, lusty shouting reaffirmed his fame, proclaiming even to the heavens that he was el número uno. In the billiard room, the terse tap of the balls seemed the essence of wealth and power; neither the mounting whine of his Maserati nor the ring of fine crystal could compare. Aside from listening to the balls collide, Paco Machismo had no interest in the game.

Around the walls of the room, the mounted heads of his more illustrious victims looked down in utter bovine stupidity. Pinned like sporty carnations to every black, muscled hump was a rosette divisa with the colors of the breeding ranch. Small brass plaques identified each animal by name and gave the time and place of the fight. Between the trophies hung enlarged framed photographs of el número uno in action, his cape swirling like the skirts of a flamenco dancer. The other photos were portraits of men whose legends he admired: Juan Belmonte, Luis Miguel Dominguín, Joe DiMaggio. Although Paco could neither read nor write, rows of leather-bound books completed the decor.

Reclining on a low divan opposite the fireplace, naked except for the tattooed butterfly splayed on her left buttock, a seventeen-year-old Irish girl named Mercy Malone, whose recording "Serendipity" was currently number nine on the pop charts back home, waited for something to happen. She nibbled at an assortment of macrobiotic goodies set on the onyx table in front of the fire: soy crackers spread with miso, radish and beansprout salad, brown rice flavored with kelp, and a steaming pot of mu tea. Paco Machismo was a dedicated vegetarian. He never ate meat of any kind.

Don Pepe found a space on the wooden bench along the white-tiled wall of the steam room. He spread his towel and settled back like a brooding hen. Rivulets of sweat coursed over the folds of his flaccid body. The empresario had once been a fat man; now, deflated by age and illness, his sagging skin seemed several sizes too large.

He closed his eyes and breathed the hot, pine-scented vapor, relaxing, when a familiar voice called, "Hola, Pepe." The empresario scrutinized the ghostly figures around him in the Hades fog until he recognized an old amigo, the mayoral on the bull-breeding ranch of the Conde de San Conejo. "Qué tal, hombre," Don Pepe said. "What brings you in off the farm?"

"Business, always business. How goes it with you?"

"Badly. I've had no luck since the death of Arturo Madrigal."

The mayoral crossed himself. "They say his tomb is a shrine now. Hundreds leave flowers every day."

Sweat dripped from Don Pepe's nose. "What good does it do me to own sixty percent of a shrine? I can't eat flowers. I've got a good boy coming along now, perhaps a little awkward, but very brave. One good break is all he needs. But what chance is there when I lack the funds for a decent bribe? I can't offer promises. The critics just laugh at me."

"Claro. The corrida is a risky life; the horns are always waiting, and even if a man lives to cut the pigtail and retire, what is there to do? His days are filled with boredom. Better to have a useful trade, like auto mechanics or guitar making. When a skill is in the fingers it never leaves you."

Don Pepe wondered if this was true. He remembered his own early years as a pickpocket and regretted the enforced nakedness of the steam room. There had been a time when he could have lifted the lint from a man's navel without a tickle. Arthritis ruled out any hope of a comeback. With those gnarled and twisted fingers, even picking his nose was something of an accomplishment.

The bull, el Camión, was feeling mean. He was in the mood for kicking ass. All day he watched the stud bulls in the next pasture, dragging their ponderous balls through the tall grass, alternately browsing with the cows and mounting them. At sundown they were still at it and the young bull stood in the golden haze with his nose pressed to the barbed wire. It made el Camión mad to watch this lordly, patient progress through the herd. They could afford to take their time; twenty-two years old and fat as sultans. None of the young fighting bulls had ever seen them even trot.

El Camión was full grown at four; six hundred kilos on the hoof and strong enough to lift a horse with a toss of his widespread horns. For three years, he had spent his days by the fence, watching the stud bulls at their pleasure. He was missing out and this made him surly. El Camión was spoiling for a fight.

In the shadows of an oak tree near the entrance to the bull-breeding ranch of the Conde de San Conejo, a runaway gypsy girl named Esmeralda Fabada quickly finished undressing and stashed the rolled bundle of her clothes in a culvert by the highway. She started for the fields across the road, a patched canvas cape folded stiffly in her arms. An extravagant globular moon lit the treeless landscape, but the gypsy girl knew the way even in the dark. Except for her rope-soled espadrilles, she was stark naked.

The cape was irreplaceable. During the day it remained hidden in the culvert. As she crossed the open field, Esmeralda wore it draped over one shoulder with her left arm wrapped and slung, in the manner of the processional entrance of the toreros into the bullring. She walked proudly, her lithe adolescent body aglow with moonlight.

Near the bank of a shallow stream she came upon the sleeping herd. The animals were settled, legs folded beneath them, cuds working even in sleep. She tiptoed behind the first hulking shadow and delivered a swift kick to the base of its spine.

The bull was up and roaring with the speed of a racehorse out of the starting gate. Immense and black, the moonbright horns lifted as the beast circled once and spotted his tormentor advancing, one sliding step at a time, behind the spread wall of canvas. The bull lowered his head and charged, a berserk boxcar of hate and fury. The gypsy girl stood, tasting blood, and passed the brute with a slow, floating veronica, so close that one stiletto horn tip left a scratch across her naked thigh.

"A brave animal," Esmeralda thought. The charge was straight and true, with none of the preliminary ground pawing that is the mark of a coward. The bull wheeled and Esmeralda passed him a second time—so close that if she'd been wearing clothes a horn would certainly have caught the garment and tossed her. On the ground, with no one to distract the bull's attention, her chances for survival would be slight. A horn thrust would pin her to the earth like a lepidopterist's specimen. The thought of the butterfly collection in the window of the Mariposa Restaurant on the Puerto del Sol was more than vivid when the moon slid behind a cloud and she could no longer see the bull.

Esmeralda heard the thunder of approaching hoofbeats. Something huge sped across her path, a rush of wind like a passing auto. The girl turned and ran. She stumbled into a dry arroyo and collided with a naked boy. They fell backward into a gorse thicket, a tangle of arms and legs and thorns.

"Caramba!" muttered the astounded boy when his flailing arm chanced to find Esmeralda's lovely breast. His amazement was punctuated by a loud wolf-wail of pain as sharp, determined teeth closed on his forearm and gnawed for bone.

"Cabrón," the gypsy girl hissed as he released her.

The boy sucked his injured arm. "Can it be you, Esmeralda?"

"You pig! What are you doing to me? I will cut your cojones off."

This was a distinct possibility and the boy, who valued his manhood too highly for such a risk, sat back on his haunches and closed his legs protectively. "What business have you here, Esmeralda?" he demanded.

"Pig!" She spat at him. "I have more skill with the cape than any of you monkeys."

"What? Have you come to cape the bulls?" The boy laughed. "Are you not afraid of the horns?"

"I am afraid of nothing."

"But what of those sharp horns, Esmeralda? When they kiss your flesh it is not so sweet as this." And he bent forward and took her hard brown nipple between his lips.

"Filthy goat!" Esmeralda twisted in his clumsy embrace, pulling her breast from his mouth.

The boy only laughed and smacked his lips, unable to take his gaze from her protruding nipple, swollen in the half-light like the cap and stem of an inverted mushroom. "I can think of better sport than caping calves," he said.

Esmeralda continued to struggle, but her efforts had an effect opposite from her intentions; her straining breasts rubbed against her aggressor's chest and evidence of his arousal was soon poking into her vulnerable tummy. "Toad," she shrieked. "Maggot-worm! Horsefly!"

"You're not afraid of it, are you, muchacha?" the boy said, diving for her bobbing breasts. "Truly, this is one horn you have no cause to fear."

"You miserable scum! I would not want you if your words were sweet and delicate as the almond blossoms. Not even if that pink puppy's weapon you act so proud of were taller and straighter than the spire of Córdoba Cathedral."

The boy's laughter stopped. "You think me s–small?" he stammered.

It was Esmeralda's turn to laugh. "Chico, my grandmother owns a rabbit with better equipment than you."

The boy's enthusiasm wilted along with his erection. "Who wants you then?" he said, getting to his feet. "But I'm working this end of the field. I've been here since dark."

"You can keep it," Esmeralda said. "I'll go to the section across the river."

"No, Basilio is practicing there tonight."

"Okay, the pasture below the olive grove."

"That is where you'll find Tomás."

"Then I'll work the calves."

"Impossible, Jesús Segundo went in that direction."

"Christ! Is the whole village out tonight?"

The clouds unveiled the moon for a moment, the tooth-paste-colored light slowly bringing the fields back into focus as if a rheostat were being turned somewhere in the central power station off behind the spiral nebula. Everywhere Esmeralda looked, the surrounding checkerboard of fenced pasture was overrun with naked boys! Boys of all shapes and sizes scurried among the thornbushes, dragging scraps of canvas or salvaged blankets. Seldom had the noble Spanish earth witnessed such a spectacle as this swarm of nakedness. A spread fan of clouds covered the face of the modest Castilian moon and discreet shadows slid into place once again.

"See," the boy whispered, standing in back of her, "there's no place to go. It would be better for you to stay here with me." The naked boy encircled her bare waist with his arms.

"Why not?" Esmeralda said, reaching behind her back. "Hmmm, I underestimated you, chico."

The boy felt her cool fingers encircle him and thrilled to the electric friction of her firm milkmaid's stroke. He closed his eyes and fumbled for her breasts, breathing her dark hair and calling her his "sweet white dove" in a tobacco-flavored whisper. Then, those loving, slender fingers closed in a vise-grip, yanking and twisting the way her grandmother wrung the necks of chickens, and his bedroom murmur built into a scream that split the night sky like an air-raid siren.

Esmeralda looked down at the writhing boy hunched in agony at her feet. "Next time, you must treat a lady with some manners, cabrón," she said. "And if the pain seems too great, perhaps you should give up your dreams of becoming a matador: a cornada in the bullring will hurt much more than this."

El Chicote stood in the shadows by the trolley stop watching a warm, well-lighted car clatter past but lacking the fare for a few hour's sleep. He hugged the embossed leather swordcase against his chest, trying not to think about park benches or the drafty ferrocarril waiting room, when a familiar voice hailed him from across the cobbled street. "Carlos, my boy," the man called, with a wave of his furled umbrella. "How long it's been." It was Señor Esteban Sanchez; *Professor* Sanchez, his old teacher, to whom he owed every particle of his skill.

"So good to see you again, Carlos," Señor Sanchez said, gripping his hand. "How many years is it now? Two? Three?"

"Almost four, Professor, but it seems like yesterday. You look just the same."

"A few additional gray hairs perhaps; I try to keep fit. How goes the career?"

"Quite well, actually. Oh, I had some bad luck Sunday, but the critics always exaggerate these things, blow them all out of proportion."

"You know I never read reviews, Carlos. Come along, have some supper with me—a little gathering in the studio like old times."

They walked along streets and alleyways progressively more sordid with each block. Garbage lay spilled across the cobbles and in the gutter; the slimy puddle that mirrored the modest Castilian moon also floated an armada of eggshells and orange peels. Several lengths of wrinkled sausage casing, the poor man's condom, lay at anchor along the curb.

A limping cat led the way as the two men crossed into a muddy courtyard. In the dismal yellow light of a low-wattage bulb hung a familiar signboard, the ornate gilt letters obscured by grime:

INSTITUTO SANCHEZ

SALON DE TAUROMACHIA

ACCEPTAMOS BANKAMERICARD

El Chicote paused for a moment and looked up at the painting of a matador performing a full veronica, so faded now that neither the bull nor the man showed. Only the red cape was still visible, like the wings of an exotic moth pausing for the night.

"Coming, Carlos?"

At the top floor, the door to the studio stood open, spilling light into the hall, and as he entered, el Chicote saw it was the same: the brick walls plastered with ragged poster-sized diagrams of the basic passes, footwork detailed along the sides like dance notation. In the center of the room stood a padded leather gymnast's horse nicknamed Rosinante, bristling with banderillas and leaking sawdust. A wheelbarrow chassis with a set of bull horns as a hood ornament waited below a curtain of faded pink capes hanging from pegs in the wall. A long table was set with bread baskets and wicker-covered demijohns of cheap red wine and numbers of noisy students sat boasting and drinking; the room was loud with angry shoptalk.

Professor Sanchez beckoned the novillero to join him by the coal stove where a lean, hollow-cheeked man in a chef's apron presided over several steaming pots. The professor bobbed up and down like a vaudeville China-man. "Carlos," he said, "I want you to meet the most talented of my recent graduates, Luis Orlando. Luis, this

21

is one of my old boys, Carlos Carretera. He is called el Chicote in the bullring now."

The consumptive Luis regarded the novillero with undisguised scorn. "I've heard of you," he said, barely moving his thin lips. "You're the one the critics call 'the Aviator' because you spend so much time in the air."

Carlos had to clear his throat. "Bah, who bothers to read the reviews? All those vermin know about bulls is how they like their beefsteak prepared."

Professor Sanchez was bobbing out of control. "Gentlemen, gentlemen, let us all be friends. This is not a time for hard words. Tonight we celebrate. Today, at a small rural feria, Luis cut both ears and the tail of his second bull."

"Congratulations," Carlos croaked unconvincingly.

"Show him," the Professor urged.

"Mira." Luis Orlando lifted the lid of the stewpot. A wreath of steam parted and revealed his simmering trophies, scraped and hairless in the golden broth.

The dark, vaulted-brick cellar in the Alma de Andalucía nightclub echoed with the plaintive nasal lament of cante jondo. Paco Machismo, el número uno, passed among the bare wood tables, nodding with grave dignity to his many admirers. Mercy Malone hung onto his left arm, looking absolutely peachy in her see-through blouse and a pair of red velvet hot pants. When the matador and his maid crossed in front of the bandstand the singer interrupted the fluty arabesques of his tortured ballad to clap his hands. Soon the guitar players were all applauding, and by the time the couple reached their reserved table the place was roaring with bravos.

The brave one's manager, Alfredo Gazpacho, stood hunched by the table, clapping with the enthusiasm of a trained seal, an unlit cigar clenched in his fawning smile.

Seated on either side like bookends in Cardin suits and matching blue-tinted sunglasses, two American strangers joined in the applause. Paco Machismo held up one hand to silence the crowd and nodded for the singer to continue. At this signal, a swarm of waiters surrounded the table, helping the illustrious pair into their seats and whisking away crumbs.

By the time the orders were taken, the singer had finished and a flurry of guitars accompanied the frenzied tapping and clapping of six swarthy dancers. His manager made the introductions but Machismo, who always had trouble with names, couldn't remember which of the plump, suntanned Americans was Marty and which was Abe. ("Mardi" and "Ape" was the way the bullfighter heard it over the noise of the flamenco troupe.) Strange names, even for Americans. He wondered if they were gangsters.

The Americans were here on business, Gazpacho explained. They had a proposition to make. Much money would be involved. At the word "dinero," Paco inched his chair imperceptibly closer. The deal was this: most of the high-paying customers at the corrida were now Americans who couldn't tell a natural from a media veronica; what they were after was thrills and excitement. They were aficionados only of danger. But with the bulls getting smaller every season and as a result of the recent horn-shaving scandal, the number of paying customers was dwindling. Something new was needed; something big.

"You want me to fight six bulls in one afternoon?" Machismo said with a snap of his fingers. "It is nothing. I fight the whole cartel by myself."

"No, Paco, this is bigger than that. This is something new." His manager paused, nodding at the two men flanking him. "Abe and Marty are motion-picture producers from Hollywood, California. They want to make a film of an entirely new spectacle and are offering you five hundred thousand American dollars—"

"That's half a million clams, sweetheart," Ape (or was it Mardi?) interjected.

"Yes, half a million," Gazpacho continued. "More than you can earn in two seasons."

"For a one-shot," the Americans shouted, almost in tandem.

"And what must I do for so much money?" Paco Machismo fixed his ball-bearing eyes on the two Americans.

"It will be in the tradition of the ancient gladiators." His manager waved his arms with enthusiasm. "Something which has not been seen. It will be the equal of the days when bears were pitted against bulls in the arena."

"You want me to fight a bear?"

"No, Paco, much bigger than a bear. Have you ever been to the zoo in the capital?"

"Never. I don't like to see animals in cages."

"Well then, here is a photo." His manager slid an eight-by-ten glossy across the table. "From Africa, Paco."

Paco Machismo stared at the picture of the prehistoric-looking creature with unconcealed amazement.

"That baby's worth half a million smackers to you, hot shot," Mardi (perhaps it was Ape) gloated. "D.O.A. Think you can handle it?"

For once in his career, el número uno was unable to come up with an answer.

After dinner, Professor Sanchez asked his two distinguished graduates to give the students a demonstration of their professional artistry. Tables and benches were pushed back against the walls for extra room. Several wineskins made the rounds. El Chicote and Luis Orlando rummaged like housewives at the flea market through the capes hanging along the wall, inspecting them all before making a selection. The fastest runner in the class was chosen to push the wheel-mounted bull horns.

The display soon developed into a mano a mano. Rowdy applause followed each pass, the students whistling and stamping, and after running through the basics, the two novilleros were encouraged to show off and take risks. The capework became more elaborate; the men inched closer and closer to the passing horns. Luis Orlando received a near ovation when two buttons were torn from his shirt front during a perfect statuesque parón.

Not to be outdone, el Chicote called for a blindfold. Professor Sanchez attempted to introduce a note of reason at this point but his protests were lost amid the students' cheers. Someone offered a denim bandana and wound it over the eyes of Carlos Carretera. The novillero held up his hand for silence. "I intend to introduce this feat in the arena," he announced. "With only the sound of the bull's hoofbeats to guide me, I perform a series of the most technically demanding passes."

The crowd fell silent as el Chicote strode to the center of the floor, dragging his cape behind him like a peacock's tail. "Hah, toro," he grunted with a stamp of the foot. At this signal, the student manning the horns began to run, pushing the wheeled contraption for all he was worth. El Chicote shook out the folded cape and began a Chicletina, pirouetting as the proxy bull charged past, the cape swirling in midair and wrapping gracefully around his body. Unfortunately the horns were passing on the wrong side, behind his back, so the stunt merely looked foolish. Even as the first laughter started, the corner of el Chicote's whirling cape caught in the wheelspokes of the fast-moving mechanism and the novillero was yanked off balance, the wrapped canvas unwinding with a snap which catapulted him across the room for a nasty nose-and-teeth landing against the leg of the dinner table.

Luis Orlando clapped his hands silently, his thin-lipped frown intact in spite of the surflike roar of student laughter. "A fine display of the style for which the Aviator is justly famous," he muttered to Professor Sanchez, standing aghast by his side.

El Camión, the fighting bull, grazed along the riverbank in the moonlight. His reflection glistened on the smooth-flowing stream. There were no flies, but every so often out of habit his tail whisked lazily across his haunches. Eating calmed the big animal and he no longer raised his red-eyed head after each bite to search the darkness for further threat.

It had been a confusing night out on the range. The centaurs who rode herd during the daytime, armed with long poles and ropes, had split apart and attacked him on two legs while he slept. Miserable puny creatures now, who tormented him and then disappeared behind a turn of cloth when attacked. El Camión knew the next time he met a two-legged he would ignore this flapping enticement and aim for his body instead.

Mercy Malone crouched on all fours in the corner on a rug made from the neck fur of three thousand arctic foxes. Her pale freckled body shone with sweat. She was out of breath, panting, her strawberry breasts dancing between her slender arms. The tattooed butterfly fluttered overhead on the ceiling mirror. Clamped on her head in the manner of earmuffs was a pair of plastic horns.

She stared up at Paco Machismo, standing by the bed

with a rawhide quirt in his hand and flinched as the thongs flickered past her shoulder. He was a beautiful sight, a Cubist arrangement of planes and angles, sun-bronzed, with a dark glossy pelt spreading across his chest and stomach, his upthrust cock bright as a candied apple.

"See him standing to like a proper little redcoat," the girl said.

"Eh? Speak Spanish," Paco Machismo grunted and gave her another short taste of the lash. "This time I will take you recibiendo."

"What in the bloody hell is that? *Ouch!* Okay, okay, qué es eso?"

"In the arena, it is the most noble achievement of a matador: to receive the bull's charge and go between the horns for the killing thrust."

"Por favor, I'm too young to die."

The torero was suddenly serious. "Oh, no, my darling, you are never too young for the dark messenger's call."

"Shit, Paco, I was only kidding. You don't have to be such a philosopher."

"I never joke about death."

"Bueno, bueno."

"I laugh at death."

"Fine."

"Ha-ha-ha; listen to that. That is what I feel for death."

"How do you feel about fucking?"

The candied apple drew itself up to full height. "It is what I enjoy second most in life."

"Swell." The Irish girl smiled at him through twin cur-tains of straight-hanging barley-colored hair. "Say the word and I'll jump you; you know, whatchamacallit, recibiendo?"

"I will receive your charge." Paco Machismo tossed the

27

whip behind him onto the bed. He pivoted on the balls of his feet, back arching from the pelvis like a strung bow, and clapped his hands twice. "Hah. Hola."

The girl broke like a sprinter at the sound of the starter's gun and covered the fox-fur rug in two seconds flat. She was on him in a single bound, her legs locked around his waist. Impaled, they staggered upright together for a momentary mantis dance before toppling over backward onto the circular bed.

miércoles

THE LOBBY OF THE HOTEL AVILA was filled with old men. They sat at tables along the blistered walls, playing dominoes in the half-light, or in sagging plush easy chairs with skirts of epaulet-fringe, relighting cigars and staring out the unwashed windows at the Street of the Knifesharpeners. Folded newspapers rested like scepters across every lap. Sporting sheets were what they read, along with the weekly bullfight periodicals, for the Hotel Avila was located in that district of the city which for a time after the civil war was popular with nine-day bicycle racers, matadors and jockeys and was now the home of the discarded of that era: aging bookmakers, decrepit sword-handlers and picadors, retired trainers and advance men.

The empresario Don Pepe had a room on the third floor of the Avila, but he was not often seen in the lobby, preferring to spend his days sitting in bars instead. His presence this morning, on the couch under the clock with one hand missing, attracted little attention. Just another old man passing time.

Don Pepe failed to leave for the barroom on schedule

because of a phone call which came for him at the desk as he was putting on his topcoat. Under other circumstances the news would have elated the empresario: the most promising novillero in Spain had been badly injured in an automobile accident and the ring management wanted someone to fill his contract next Sunday. But the old man had only el Chicote in his stable, and the boy needed easy fights in the country to get his nerve back up. Signing him for another appearance in the Municipal Arena with its thirty-arroba bulls and unbribable officials would be to seal his death warrant. Worse, Don Pepe would be left without anyone to manage. The prospect of all those idle days in the lobby of the Avila made him place a somewhat higher value on the life of Carlos Carretera than the market warranted.

As he sat pondering his decision, Don Pepe flipped through a pile of old *Life* magazines. Occasionally, sexy photos eluded the Government censors. He almost skipped an article in the science section, only stopping for a second glance because a fighting bull was pictured. The empresario knew how Archimedes felt that day in the tub. There, on the glossy, dog-eared page before him was the answer to all his problems.

The most impressive monument in the graveyard outside the Extremaduran town of Sueño de Duende was a white marble wedding cake whose Corinthian columns and trumpeting angels covered what was left of a previous answer to all of Don Pepe's problems. After only three seasons, Arturo Madrigal had been proclaimed the "successor to Manolete" by a cautious and cynical press. Bookings arrived from every part of the peninsula. Don Pepe made a down payment on a black Chrysler Ambassador barely nine years old. That particular bubble burst along with Arturo Madrigal's liver and spleen one windy April Sunday in Málaga when a sudden gust lifted the boy's cape and the left horn of a Cordoba bull named el Osario caught him below the rib cage.

A life-sized effigy of the young matador in his suit of lights adorned the lid of the columned sarcophagus, floral bouquets blanketing his marble image. Wherever the sculptor portrayed flesh (hands clasped in prayer, an innocent choirboy face) the statue was tinted the color of boiled shrimp. Unlike the ancient Greeks, who colored their sculpture for greater realism, art played no part in this; Arturo Madrigal's cheeks and fingers were pink with smudged lipstick. Several thousand furtive kisses had conspired to produce this caricature of life's bloom.

A black angel presided unseen above all the post-mortem adulation, her features stern as a gyrfalcon's. From her aerie in the bell tower, Arturo Madrigal's mother watched the steady procession of mourners through war-surplus German field glasses. She memorized the face of every visitor to the graveyard, sorting the strangers from townspeople with legitimate dead and keeping a mental tally of all the hysterical women who caressed her son's tomb. Those who came but once were quickly forgotten. Should they return, even a year later, on the anniversary of Arturo's death, the grim yellow eyes would narrow in recognition and hatred.

Mercy Malone carried a pot of Irish breakfast tea into the library. The jellaba she wore was several sizes too large. It was a trophy acquired on a trip to Marrakech with King Hassan's Minister of Transport, and her nifty schoolgirl's figure was lost beneath its tentlike folds. She left Paco sleeping upstairs, his body spread in an X-shape which quadrisected the circular bed like the figure in

Leonardo's study of anatomical proportion. Mercy had seen the Leonardo drawing in one of the library's uncut leatherbound volumes. The figure was as multilimbed as a Hindu deity, arms and legs in a variety of postures. There had only been one fig leaf, a detail Mercy noticed straightaway. This did little to prevent further speculation and the Irish pop star spent that particular afternoon dreaming of six-legged men with triple erections.

Mercy was the only person who ever used the Machismo library for anything other than shooting billiards or admiring dead meat. She enjoyed looking at books—old books with creepy engravings. In her London apartment, a soundless television flickered unwatched in a corner while Mercy sprawled on the carpet, smoking hash through a rum-filled Turkish hookah, surrounded by magazines, comic books, Agatha Christies, selected pornography and the works of Dickens (a long-term project).

Doing "one-potato, two-potato" along the top shelf, Mercy picked a Greek mythology illustrated with lithographic plates. She sat by the fire, poured out a cup of tea and opened the book on her lap. Chance provided the tale of Zeus abducting Europa. She turned a protective tissue-paper page and studied the picture. The woman with the plump thighs and small breasts didn't seem at all to mind the attentions of the powerful horned beast standing, black and mountainous, above her. A *bull!* Mercy Malone was simply goggle-eyed. She gazed up at the mounted trophies around the room and felt a shudder of accelerating delight ascend her spine.

"Name?"
"Carlos Carretera."
"Age?"
"Twenty-five."

"Address: none. Occupation?"

"Matador de toros."

The captain rubbed first his eyes, then his mustache, and looked at the disheveled man standing on the other side of the desk. "A dangerous line of work," he said. On the cardboard admission form he typed NO VISIBLE MEANS OF SUPPORT. "Is this your identity card?"

"Yes. The address is my father's. It will do you no good to contact him."

"We already have. He's never heard of you. Says he has no son."

"It is I who no longer have a father."

The captain's expression could not be described as a smile. On the corner of the ink-stained blotter lay his .9 mm Browning automatic. The portraits of his wife and sons across the desk and of the Generalissimo, hanging aslant from the pale green wall above, were placed so that the pistol's reflection showed in the glass. This was the captain's favorite trick. The clip in the automatic was empty, unlike the cylinder of the snub-nosed .38 caliber Smith & Wesson police special waiting in the top drawer of the desk. It was surprising how many takers he got. Enough in the past year to earn the captain three unit citations, one signed by the Comandante himself.

But this prisoner ignored the bait; would not in fact even look at the pistol or its many reflections. The captain continued typing for a space or two on the platen after he finished the form, and when that didn't work, he bent down and pretended to search for a sheet of escaped carbon paper under the typewriter stand. He heard Carlos Carretera clear his throat but rose to find him rocked back on his heels, staring at the ceiling. "Private!" he called, placing the admission form in a manila folder.

The man with the tommy gun who appeared in the

open doorway had a face so serious that even the sideways, patent-leather hat he wore did not seem foolish. "Sir?"

"Show the torero the accommodations."

"Si, mi capitán."

Perhaps the poorest resident in any rural village is the local cobbler. Most villagers cannot afford shoes; often a single pair serves an entire family, coming off the shelf at most twice a year, and only for such important occasions as weddings and funerals. A mother might see all her sons married in the same boots her husband had worn to the altar. There is not much work for a cobbler in such a town.

When Esmeralda Fabada entered the shop, the old cobbler did not even bother to look up, ignoring the clatter of goat bells hanging on the door. He was busy pasting colored pictures clipped from a *National Geographic* magazine onto the whitewashed walls. Between the hanging hammers, knives and awls were views of the palace at Knossos, bare-breasted Kikuyu tribeswomen, the Great Wall of China, Polynesians spearing fish by torchlight, a snow leopard crouching, assorted butterflies and tropical beetles.

The swirl of a pleated skirt interrupted the work at hand. Esmeralda kissed the old cobbler on the cheek. "Buenos días, viejo," she said.

The shoemaker showed the girl his new pictures of Venezuela. "Would you like to go to the New World and see butterflies as large as umbrellas?" he asked.

"Perhaps someday, a tour of the Americas . . ."

"Butterflies so big a man could ride on one."

"Oh, Uncle, your imagination carries you away with it."

"The world is a place of miracles: fish that climb trees, whales heavier than locomotives, birds that fly all the way from Africa each year. These things do not come from the imagination. I have seen fotos. Only the mind of God could imagine such wonders."

"I don't believe in miracles," the gypsy girl said.

"And what else is there?"

"Deeds!"

The old cobbler placed the glue pot on a shelf. "Then how can I help you?"

"I need some work done. A pair of slippers."

"Muy bien. I must draw the outline of your feet. Here." He placed a sheet of brown paper on the floor. "Stand here." His pencil traced the delicate contour of her arch. "Are these to be dancing slippers?"

"No."

"Tell me then, what sort of slippers?"

"Bullfighting slippers. Zapatillas de torera. Make them without heels as is the custom."

The old cobbler looked at the ceiling. "A young girl walks into my shop and asks for bullfighting slippers, and she says she doesn't believe in miracles."

"How much do you charge?"

"Four hundred pesetas."

"I will pay half now." Esmeralda counted out the coins and stacked them on the workbench. "When will they be ready?"

"Tomorrow afternoon, if you are in a hurry."

"It is you who should hurry."

"You can have them tonight!"

"There is more profit in this than pasting pictures on the wall, old man." The girl turned at the entrance. "I will return at eleven."

The slamming door started the string of goat bells

jangling with such violence it sounded as if whole herds were stampeding. "That one is fire and wind," the old cobbler said, holding the map of her feet in his hands.

Doña Carlota Madrigal lowered her binoculars and covered her ears with her hands. Floor planks trembled underfoot as the tolling noon bell dislodged a cloud of rock doves from the tower's tracery. The birds whirled out over the graveyard, turning in a single motion like a dark school of airborne fish.

Below in the churchyard, the solitary mourner was little troubled by the reverberating bells. She lay prostrate, hugging the marble image of Arturo Madrigal, a coil of rolled stocking showing where her skirt was hiked above her plump knee.

When the echoes died and the doves returned to their nooks in the tower, the sobbing señora gave the statue a final lingering kiss before sitting up to tug at her disheveled clothing and dab her moist eyes. After three consecutive visits, she had this private gravestone dry hump well timed, and knew from experience that late morning was when the cemetery was most often deserted. It was best to take no chances after midday. The crunching approach of footsteps in the gravel reaffirmed her precaution.

She glanced up at a gaunt, yellow-eyed woman in long black skirts and an embroidered apron, a basket of wild flowers on her arm, field glasses in a leather case by her side. "Por favor," the woman said, "I bring these few blossoms for my son." Doña Carlota made the sign of the cross and knelt by the tomb, scattering a handful of petals across the polished effigy.

The other mourner found it difficult to reply. "Arturo's . . . m–madre?" she stammered.

"Sí. I am Señora Carlota Madrigal." The tall woman in black rose stiffly to her feet.

"Ah, señora, your son was every fiber a man."

"He was very brave."

"Muy hombre. And yet so innocent, still a boy."

"You have seen Arturo work the bulls?"

"Many times. He fought in Sevilla twelve times his second season. Each appearance was a triumph."

"Would you like to see some photographs taken that year? My house is not far from the church."

"Oh, Señora Madrigal, I would consider it an honor."

"I have a cocido on the stove, Arturo's favorite. When you break bread you are no longer strangers."

Don Pepe Bacalao y Piñas hurried across the crowded avenue, a dog-eared copy of *Life* clamped under his arm. He turned left at the monument to Alfonso VII and continued past the Moorish façade of the poultry market into a district of secondhand shops and winding cobbled streets. Old black-shawled women holding straw baskets piled with asparagus sat on the curb crying mournfully for customers. Numbers of emaciated dogs nosed along the sidewalk, greeting each new smell with a lifted leg.

At the entrance to a building at one time a cork warehouse but now divided into narrow, squalid apartments hung rows of birdcages, the property of an elderly white-haired barber who operated a small shop on the ground floor. Don Pepe paused in the doorway and called to the man, busy stropping a razor inside. He had to yell to make himself heard above the raucous cries of caged macaws, mynahs, nightingales, meadowlarks, chimney swifts, goatsuckers, thrushes, linnets, canaries, condors, buntings, martins, toucans and lovebirds: "Is the Chinaman at home?"

"Sí, señor," the barber answered, not missing a stroke. "Upstairs."

Don Pepe's murmured "Gracias" was lost among the burbling birdsong. "Long live death. Long live death," a parrot screamed above the uproar.

The empresario wheezed his way up the steep stone stairs. As a rule the fat old man avoided any exertion, and with good reason, but today he was risking cerebral hemorrhage or worse, for of all his many friends in the city, only his trusted Chinese buddy, Lucky Sam Wo, could help him now.

Don Pepe had known Lucky Sam for forty-four years, since the dictatorship of Primo de Rivera, when the ingenious Oriental first arrived in the country accompanied by a Turkish wife and a Paraguayan passport. From the start they had done business together. Lucky Sam sold the empresario (then operating under the sobriquet Manitos de Oro) a pair of mechanical arms which, inserted through the sleeves of a topcoat, could be made to hold an umbrella or a book and even to turn pages. This device greatly added to Don Pepe's early fortunes, for while the mechanical hands thumbed a volume of Unamuno on a crowded trolley, the empresario's own golden fingers were busy in the pockets of his fellow passengers.

Clearly, Lucky Sam Wo was a genius. Over the years, his inventions had figured in every major crime on the Iberian peninsula and many of his creations were used by the Continental underworld in capers as far away as Poland and Scandinavia. The Black Museum of Scotland Yard had on display no less than nine of the Chinese wonder's more notable toys, including: a stethoscopelike contrivance that enabled even rank amateurs to dial unknown safe combinations, a magnetic apparatus capable of immobilizing the most sensitive burglar alarm, a revolver disguised as a banana, and a portable printing press, carried in a lady's hatbox, which converted ten-pound notes into hundred-pound notes at the turn of a crank.

The door to Wo's workshop/apartment was partway open and the empresario entered without knocking, experiencing the same rush of innocence and wonder which assaulted him whenever he came here. It was like a return to childhood. Everything was unfamiliar and mysterious. As with most civilized men, the act of switching on an electric light was for Don Pepe a miracle merely taken for granted, but when confronted by this humming, blinking roomful of complex machinery he was properly awed.

The sounds of a radio broadcast led him through the mechanical labyrinth to a workbench in the rear where he found Lucky Sam probing with a soldering iron among the tangled intestines of a disabled machine. Distracted by the empresario's shadow, the Oriental inventor glanced up through a green plastic eyeshade with visible annoyance, but his frown turned instantly to a grin of pleasure at the sight of his old comrade. "Hola, Pepito," he said. "Como 'stá, hombre?" Lucky Sam spoke Spanish with a pure Castilian accent completely free of any music-hall sing-song. "Come. I have a new creation it will give me great pleasure to show you." The Chinaman escorted his visitor back through the maze of esoteric appliances to a raised wooden platform on which hulked something monstrous, draped with a canvas drop cloth like a statue before its unveiling. "It is you who are the inspiration for this work, Pepe."

"Me?"

"Cómo no? Remember, two years ago at the San Isidro festival we had a discussion about why the corrida was unacceptable to North Americans? We agreed it wasn't the violence: Yankees love violence. Look at boxing. Look at American football. American football is the most violent sport in the world. Every year more young men are killed and maimed on the gridiron than in the bullring. Statistics prove this: It is safer to be a matador than a quarterback. And yet, Americans love football and hate the corrida. Why? Because of the bull. The bull suffers and is killed. Yankees are very sensitive about animals. They have beauty shops for their dogs. Societies keep you from beating your horse."

"Claro. I would rather be a poodle in the United States than a black man."

"Eso, es, Pepe, yet look at the number of Yankee tourists who go to bullfights. If only the bull wasn't hurt there would be a great audience for the corrida in the United States. Millions could be made. However, without the moment of truth there is nothing, an empty spectacle. The problem was, how to keep the moment of truth, the danger and violence, and at the same time not harm the bull."

"And what was your solution, Sammy?"

"Mira." Lucky Sam Wo yanked away the canvas dropcloth and revealed his remarkable invention. The head was very much that of a bull; small, staring eyes, a wide pair of curved, gleaming horns, flared nostrils that seemed almost to breathe; but the rest of the body was clearly a machine: a taurine robot. Cog wheels, gears, and cables connected to tubular steel; ganglionic complexes of wires, transistors, circuitry and switches took the place of vital organs; oil glistened on ball bearings and cams.

"Of course," Sam Wo said, "when the padded muscles are attached and the hide sewn in place, it will look just like the real thing. The machine carries its own computer. No live bull is as brave. It is programmed to charge straight and true. And when the sword is inserted in the neck it strikes a cutoff switch and the machine drops in its tracks."

"Estupendo!" The empresario clapped his hands three times for emphasis.

"I have achieved verisimilitude. Inside, a plastic bladder filled with red liquid enables the beast to vomit blood when wounded. Tubes lead to the shoulders and neck so the pic and banderillas will also draw blood. The liquid is my own formula and very realistic. Not even a surgeon could tell it from the genuine article."

"You are amazing, Sam, truly."

"The best part about my invention is its economy. Now the ring management will be able to use the same bull over and over again."

"I cannot find words to describe my admiration. I am speechless, amigo." The words which Don Pepe really couldn't find were the ones which would politely change the subject. While Lucky Sam Wo pressed a series of buttons, causing his robot bull to raise and lower its head, paw the ground, and moo (with the volume raised it became a bellow, but the neighbors complained), the empresario grunted with appreciation, looking for a way out. "Fantástico . . . magnífico . . . eh, maravilloso! Sam, I would not believe it if I were not seeing it with my own eyes. It is a wonder. I know of no one else, living or dead, not Westinghouse, not Faraday, not even the great Edison himself, who can rival your achievements; and that is why, Sam, I come to you for help."

Sam Wo switched off the wagging tail. "What sort of help do you need, Pepito?"

"I will explain. Two days ago, Sevillano Chico was hurt in a car crash and the arena management have come to me for a replacement. My problem is that I have only Chicote under contract at the moment. He fought last

43

Sunday and was disastrous; another appearance against these big bulls here in the capital would finish him for good."

"A simple matter, Pepe," Sam Wo said. "We can rig a hollow banderilla to operate like a syringe. Ten thousand ccs of sodium pentothal should do the trick."

"No. Drugs are no good. The officials would know in a minute something was wrong. I have a better idea."

"Ah, then why come to me, Pepe?" The Chinaman shrugged.

"Because only your genius can make it work. Here, look at this." Don Pepe opened the copy of *Life* to a well-marked spot; a two-page spread in the science section with photos of a Yale University professor facing a fighting bull alone in the arena. The professor looked particularly vulnerable in his gray businessman's suit. The bull, a Miura, stood transfixed less than twenty feet away. The article dealt with the psychosurgical control of violent behavior. Electrodes had been implanted in the bull's brain and the professor could immobilize the animal in mid-charge merely by pressing a button on his radio transmitter.

"Yes, José Delgado," Lucky Sam Wo said. "I've read of his work in ESB technology."

"Well?" Don Pepe was impatient. "Can you do it?"

"Can I do what?"

"Can you build one of those little things like he's got?"

"Of course, it's a simple matter; a few transistors, some electrodes—nothing to it."

"What about sticking it in the brain, can you do that?"

"I don't see why not. There's a diagram right here in the magazine. Some local anesthesia is all it would take."

Don Pepe was exultant. "Gracias, Sam, I'm in business again. I will split the purse with you fifty-fifty."

Lucky Sam Wo looked inscrutable. "But what of the sharp-eyed officials, Pepe?" he said. "What will they think of all those little wires sticking out of the bull's head?"

"No problem, Sam, you already have the solution to that one."

"I have?"

"Seguramente. Let me show you." The empresario, grunting like a weight lifter, eased his bulk up onto the platform and pulled the artificial mane and scalp off the machine-tooled head of the mechanical bull. "Mira. What does a vain man do when he loses his hair? El toro will look as good as new wearing a toupee!"

The vaqueros of the breeding ranch of the Conde de San Conejo rode silently across the sloping meadow, driving the steers before them. They were somber men, dressed in short leather jackets and wide-brimmed, flat-crowned hats. Coiled lariats hung from the pommels of their saddles. The noon sun glinted on the long steel tips of a dozen lances. Years of working under the fierce Iberian sky had marked them; their stern faces were as brown and wrinkled as walnuts.

The mayoral was dressed in much the same fashion as the other men but instead of a lance he carried a short braided quirt to emphasize his almost feudal authority. As overseer of the ranch, his commands were limited to monosyllables; more frequently, he merely gestured with the quirt. A brusque wave signaled the start of the drive and the vaqueros urged the steers down to the pasture where the fighting bulls grazed.

El Camión lifted his head to watch his docile, castrated brothers move among the herd, cowbells clanging. He trusted their slow movements, calmed by their placid, sexless presence, and he followed without hesitation as

45

they lured him away from the riverbank. Unlike the other fighting bulls, he never struck at the steers with his horns. The bells they wore around their necks seemed a sign of some important bovine office, a symbol as potent as the mayoral's quirt, and el Camión was willingly led by any beast who made so un-animal a noise.

The vaqueros rode among the herd, prodding with their lances, separating those animals destined for the ring from the others. El Camión watched these centaurs closely. For the moment, they were in control, but the fighting bull knew their secret. He was waiting for the time when they came apart and walked on two legs. When that happened, he would kill them.

Abe Wasserman was one of those individuals whose appearance improved when he talked on the telephone. It had to do with the relationship of nose and chin. The telephone was a prop he was comfortable with; he carried it tucked under his chin like a violin. Abe was a telephone virtuoso. "What time did you say that was?" he shouted into the instrument. "Yeah? And it got off okay? No trouble with the longshoremen?" Abe cupped his hand over the receiver. "Harry says they unloaded last night."

"Ask him why didn't he call us then?" Marty Farb said, pouring them both another scotch.

"Hello, Harry? Where is it now? . . . Where? . . . You're sure? . . . That's great. Go get drunk. . . . Okay, then go get more drunk. Speak to you tonight."

"So?" Marty put his feet up on the bed. "Where is it now?"

"You'll never fucking believe it: on the northbound train that left Valencia at six this morning. I'll call the Count right away so he can get things ready on the ranch.

Remind me to ring room service for more ice when I'm done."

The phone rang.

"I'll get it, Marty, relax." Abe was waiting on the second ring, but he let it go two more before picking up the phone. "Hello, Toro Productions, Abe Wasserman speaking. . . . I was wondering when you'd ever call, where are you now? . . . Inna hospital! You're not hurt, are you? . . . Oh, yeah, crippled kids, great publicity, ball players do it all the time in the States. Listen, I'll tell you straight right now, we're thinking of getting ourselves another boy." Abe covered the receiver. "It's the toreador."

"Tell him to go fuck himself."

"Paco, old amigo, don't keep me in suspense any longer, are you in or out? . . . Okay, that's terrific. We forgive you for sitting on your ass so long. I'll send a messenger over with the contracts this afternoon. . . . Ten percent in advance when you sign. . . . Beautiful, Paco, it's great doing business with you."

Mercy Malone continued her research. With Paco off visiting an orphanage and two children's hospitals (the type of public appearance where Mercy's no-bra niftiness was definitely not an asset), she was left alone in the library all day. In her opinion, it was worlds better than facing those frowning nuns.

Books on Greek mythology were stacked along the cushions of the billiard table and Mercy lay behind this Maginot Line of knowledge wearing nothing but granny glasses and her tattoo. The green felt stretched beneath her pale nakedness like a comic-strip bathtub.

She read of King Minos in a dozen books, fascinated by

47

Theseus' undercover mission to save the Athenian maidens, of his love affair with Ariadne; Daedalus' labyrinth; the Minotaur. Mercy couldn't get enough of the Minotaur. She swooned at the image of him roaming his shadowy maze; the shaggy, horned head and Charles Atlas body. Somewhere around the tunnel's bend, Athenian maidens trembled, waiting to be devoured.

Most of all, Mercy was intrigued by Pasiphaë. In comparison, the true confessions of Ariadne seemed strictly Grade B. Ariadne was a jerk and got ditched on the island to prove it. If Dionysus hadn't come along later she wouldn't be worth a second glance. But Pasiphaë, A's mother, was a woman Mercy found exciting. She read again and again the part where the Queen stole from the bed of Minos of Crete to amuse herself in the stables with a bull. Mercy Malone could appreciate such appetites.

From his table in the corner of the barroom, Don Pepe observed the passing crowd like a satrap enthroned. His proprietary manner fluctuated in relation to his bar bill; the more he owed, the more regal he became. When his credit was good, the empresario's patrician bearing eased and he was once again the jocular, back-slapping bourgeois businessman beloved by all. But, with his wristwatch sitting in the pawnshop window alongside the cufflinks and garnet stickpin, Don Pepe nursed his glass of manzanilla, taking short, princely sips, unapproachable as the Bourbon pretender.

Those privileged to sit at his table were all lackeys of one form or another. These included not only out-of-work toreros but also numerous small-time crooks—fellow felons from days gone by, grown old in prison and currently retired without any pension other than what they earned from Don Pepe on Sundays as sword-handlers and water boys. For this they served as the empresario's eyes and ears. The less intelligent were mere errand boys. Others, like Angus McHaggis, an eighty-two-year-old Scots confidence man who had made millions along the French Riviera in the Twenties, were trusted with more delicate missions.

When McHaggis entered the bar, he did so smiling like a man who knows his information is worth at least three drinks. "Hola, Don Pepe," he called. "Qué tal?" The marriage of his Scots burr and the baby-talk lisp of Castilian produced a sound not unlike the mating call of the reciprocating steam engine.

"Bien, bien. Sit down, mi camarada, I've been expecting you." The empresario held his breath, resisting the inevitable invitation. On the exhale he managed to say it: "What will you drink?"

"A brandy."

"Mozo! A copita of Fundador for my friend."

McHaggis waited until the glass was set in front of him and took a first grateful sip before speaking again. "Pepe, I found your boy."

"Where is he?"

Another sip. "Locked in the carcel."

"What's the charge?"

"Vagrancy. The fine they're asking is one thousand pesetas, but I think the captain will settle for seven hundred and fifty."

"Pues, it is money which must be spent, but if I spring him now I'll have to pay for his food and lodging; the carcel is free. Beans and bread will fill his belly and I'll know the kid is keeping out of trouble and where I can find him. Come see me Saturday morning and I'll have the money for the fine."

"Any messages you want delivered?" McHaggis asked when Don Pepe signaled for another drink.

"Tell him to keep in shape; he has a booking this Sunday. And to stay away from those who carry knives as surely as he avoids the horns of bulls."

The mayoral of the ranch of the Conde de San Conejo stood on the station platform holding a gold pocket watch. First the train had arrived twenty minutes late; then it took another fifteen to load and unload the baggage and mail; now, with almost an hour gone, the crate had yet to move off the uncoupled flatcar.

A creaking of pulleys was in the air. Bare-armed and sweating, the men hauled on the ropes like pyramid builders. At last the crate began to move, soaped wooden skids squealing under its weight. The mayoral closed the lid of his watch. He approached the houselike side of the crate and touched the tips of his fingers to the splintered, salt-bleached planks. It seemed as if the crate itself had sailed from Africa and that he was fingering the hull of some improbable ship. Inside, he could hear the thing moving.

Esmeralda Fabada stood in the shadows of an alleyway across the plaza and watched the American sailors gamble, a huddle of white uniforms distinct in the gathering dusk. The cries and shouts of their gaming carried across the silent cobbles,

"Eighter from Decatur."

"Boxcars."

"Snake-eyes."

"Baby needs a new pair of shoes."

Dice rattled like dancers' feet on the stones of the sleeping Spanish town. Esmeralda waited, listening to the money change hands. She knew a few words of English, enough to sell postcards and wilted wild flowers to the tourists who passed through Boca de Cabro. Although much of the crapshooters' slang was meaningless to her, she understood "Baby needs a new pair of shoes." She thought of the zapatillas being stitched by the cobbler and of the two hundred pesetas she needed to pay for them. Her need for a new pair of shoes was certainly as great as that of the sailor's baby.

Esmeralda tossed her wild black hair and pulled the top of her bodice down to show more of her breasts. She had often cursed God for giving her a woman's body, but tonight she offered a quiet prayer of thanks. The rustle of paper money across the plaza was like the sound of fire rushing through dry grass.

The jagged bottoms of broken bottles and jars glistened along the top of the high wall surrounding Señora Carlota Madrigal's estate. Her thick wooden gate was nine feet tall and studded with iron spikes. Armored behind these walls was a house built of scrolled ironwork and glass, arched greenhouses and arboretums extending from a central domed solarium. Although the night air was chilly and dry, inside the glass house steampipes and sprinklers produced an atmosphere as hot and humid as the tropics.

Señora Madrigal sat beside her guest at a carved oak table in the solarium, describing the snapshots in a family album. She kept her hands folded quietly in her lap. "That is Arturo in the Galápagos, during the last winter of his life. The tortoise he was riding he named Seneca. The initials of Captain Cook's first officer are carved on the shell."

"Amazing."

"You can see for yourself, the creature lives in our cactus and succulent garden."

"No, es verdad?"

"Sí. Herpetology was Arturo's passion, just as plants and flowers are mine. Dígame, Señora Lopez, did you come here from Sevilla by yourself?"

Señora Lopez blushed. "Oh, Doña Carlota, it is my secret. I am a widow like you are and live alone. My husband's family thinks I have gone to Mallorca for a seaside holiday."

"Your secret is safe with me. Now, the photo on the bottom shows Arturo milking venom from a diamondback rattlesnake sent by an American friend in Florida."

"Your son had the courage of a thousand, señora."

"For Arturo, fear did not exist."

Señora Lopez quavered. "What is that?" she piped, pointing a trembling finger.

Carlota Madrigal smiled. "A reticulated python, the world's second-longest snake." She stood and reached for the serpent and it moved sinuously up her arm to coil about her shoulder. "El Cid is only a baby, nine feet long."

Señora Lopez was quite plainly horrorstruck. "Does it bite?" she whimpered.

"Never. Would you like to see my orchids?"

"Yes, yes, certainly, Señora Madrigal, it would be a pleasure."

"Another glass of wine first?"

"No, gracias, three is my limit. Very good wine, muy seco."

"It is from my own vineyards. Come, the orchids are this way. Venga." Carlota Madrigal, wearing the python like a scarf across her shoulders, led Señora Lopez into a long, arched greenhouse where rows of plants with leaves as broad as mill blades glistened and dripped. At the center of the room, six vine-draped lignum vitae trees were planted in wooden tubs set around a deep circular pool. Hundreds of orchids grew in vials attached to the mossy trunks. Señora Lopez stopped and peered into the shadowy pool. "I saw something move in there," she said.

"Crocodiles. Arturo brought back five from Ethiopia years ago when he was still a schoolboy. Now, these flowers are not only lovely but also very rare. They belong to a subspecies not yet classified."

Señora Lopez groped for her companion's arm. "Excuse me, Señora Madrigal, I feel dizzy, like I'm on a boat."

"Here." Carlota Madrigal took the trembling woman by the waist. "Here is a bench. You must sit down."

Señora Lopez slumped onto the bench. "I think it was something I ate."

"Impossible. We both had the same thing and I feel nothing." Doña Carlota reached into the pocket of her apron and felt the pommel of the long double-edged puntilla. In the bullring this razor-sharp instrument delivered the *coup de grâce* to mortally wounded animals.

"I have cramps," Señora Lopez moaned. "It hurts and my head swims."

"Bend your head between your knees and you will feel better," Doña Carlota said. "You will see; a few moments and it will pass." She gripped the hilt of the dagger in her pocket as the woman bent obediently before her. Señora Lopez' dyed red hair parted when she stooped, revealing a pale white portion of the back of her neck.

Unlike his manager the empresario, Carlos Carretera had never been in jail. The young novillero expected a roomful of perverts and cutthroats, anticipating the guards' jokes as they fed him to the wolves. His mind was

53

made up: he would rather die than be raped. El Chicote was saddened at the thought that his beautiful corpse would never be photographed lying in state in the arena infirmary. The stainless-steel tables and long metal filing cabinets of the police morgue lacked the necessary ambiente.

When he was locked in an empty holding-cell, the novillero's relief was so great that the first twenty minutes of incarceration were spent crouching over the sewer drain. El Chicote regretted his hasty bowels; flushing was impossible without water and the ripe smell of excrement was no less unpleasant for being his own.

Carlos slouched on the bench, holding his breath. A list of rules was painted on the far wall but the light was too dim for the unhappy matador to make out the letters. In any case, he didn't feel like reading. When he was five, his mother had punished him by locking him in the basement. Now, twenty years later, Carlos the man experienced the same choking, constricted loneliness which had gripped a little boy trapped in the dark. And just like the little boy, el Chicote was crying.

It was a dark, windy night with roiling storm clouds obscuring a gibbous moon. Two hours before dawn, Esmeralda Fabada tied her canvas cape around her shoulders for warmth and started onto the bull-breeding ranch of the Conde de San Conejo. She was certain that at this hour all her rivals were home in bed. In one hand the gypsy girl carried a kerosene lantern. If the moon refused to cooperate, she would provide her own light for working the bulls. In her other hand she held her brand-new zapatillas.

The main pasture lay on the other side of a ten-acre marsh, and to save time, Esmeralda pushed through the tall grass, her bare feet bogging to the ankles at every step. Halfway across, the girl stopped to listen. The sound was unmistakably like the grunting of a pig: an enormous pig; a pig bigger than a diesel truck. Then the splashing of giant footfalls. Whatever it was, was running. Esmeralda listened, not daring to move. The snorting and splashing grew louder out of the darkness. At the last moment, Esmeralda closed her eyes, but not before glimpsing a passing shadow larger than the armored cars the army paraded on the anniversary of the siege of the Alcázar. It was the biggest animal the girl had ever seen in her life.

domingo

Two SOLDIERS HERDED the onlookers back away from the balcony when the bullfight crowd arrived. The empresario was among the delegates, accompanied by a picador and two veteran stickmen. They stood at the rail and looked down at the bulls in the corral below. Long rounds of arbitration and secret discussion ensued as they evaluated the animals to be fought that afternoon and grouped them in pairs of opposites, the strongest with the weakest, large and small, the longest horns with the shortest. This done, a banderillero took a packet of cigarette papers and drew off three leaves, writing the numbers of each pair with the stub of a pencil. A vaquero handed over his round Andalusian hat, and one by one the banderillero rolled the papers into tiny balls and dropped them in. Don Pepe's beret served as a cover as everyone gave the hat a shake or two for luck. The drawing followed the order of the matadors' seniority, and as el Chicote would be the last to appear, Don Pepe's was the third hand in the hat.

The empresario took his pellet of paper off where the

others couldn't see and slowly unrolled it. For once he was calm, the outcome of no importance. Whatever fate brought would be subject to the same modification. This one was signed, sealed and delivered. He looked at the printed numbers—74 and 119—and checked them against the list the ring management had given him. The bull's names were Vibora and el Camión. Their weights were listed, too. He had drawn the heaviest and the smallest. The big one, "the Truck," would go first, but not before some repair work was done under his hood.

The topaz eyes of lizards and snakes watched over Doña Carlota Madrigal as she tended her indoor gardens. A slithering of serpents surrounded every task. Her dead son's reptile collection was her only company and she was comforted by its cold-blooded presence. Her movements adopted a sinuous grace and she performed miracles with plants and flowers, her every gesture a caress. Often, while trimming or transplanting, she would stop, her hand poised in midair, and stare into the distance, lost in snakelike concentration. Not even the torpid rattler, coiled behind a glass partition, sat any stiller.

After the animals had fed they would lie motionless for hours, even days. Once, when the python escaped, it ate the neighbor's goat and didn't move for six months. Doña Carlota found this reptilian languor infectious. The sight of sleeping crocodiles stretched like tree trunks in the shallow pool filled her with tranquility. Their stillness was bliss. The lidded slivers of their eyes held the promise of eternal peace.

There was no movement among the crocodiles. The brutes were well gorged and would sleep the day away. When night came they would finish their feast in darkness and silence. The pink curve of a rib cage and one gnawed thigh were all that showed above the muddy surface of the pond.

Stripped to bra and panties, Esmeralda Fabada did her Royal Canadian Air Force exercises in front of a long mirror attached to the closet door. Chief Petty Officer Hooper's shore leave ended at eight bells and Esmeralda had the hotel room to herself until noon. She had good reason to be grateful to the military of many nations. Her new red skirt, hanging in the closet to save it from wrinkles, was a gift from a sergeant in the 103rd Highland Fusiliers. Every time she touched her toes she remembered the gray-haired lieutenant colonel, his face as red as the maple-leaf decal on his luggage, who first taught her how. And that's not all she remembered, for laced on her feet were brand-new zapatillas and every toe-touch called to mind ten stalwart members of the Atlantic fleet.

Esmeralda was in fine shape, her muscles firm and ready. She slapped her hard, flat stomach. Not an extra ounce of fat anywhere. On a whim, she ran to the dresser and seized a dime-store tube of fuchsia-colored lipstick and very carefully, with only the mirror's reverse image to guide her, she printed the words LA FABALITA across her taut tummy, dotting the *i* with a five-pointed star.

Lucky Sam Wo was dressed in his Sunday best: two-tone black-and-white shoes, red silk cravat, pin-striped double-breasted suit, the ox yoke and arrows of the Falange pinned to his wide lapel. In his right hand he carried a black leather doctor's examination bag. At the corner, he stopped and checked the time on his pocket watch with the clock in a jewelry-store window before crossing the wide avenue encircling the Plaza de Toros.

He got through the main gate without any trouble, but

a policeman was stationed at the entrance to the corrals and stables. Lucky Sam flipped open his billfold and flashed an impressive piece of forged identification. "Ministry of Agriculture," he barked. "Official business."

"What sort of business is that?"

"Veterinary examination: horn measurement, blood tests, saliva samples; the works. You will have to sign this form when I'm finished, officer."

The policeman clicked his heels and waved Sam Wo inside with a hand motion he had learned directing traffic. "You will find me at my post, Señor Doctor."

"Good." Lucky Sam paused on the ramp leading down to the stables. "No one else is to come through until I have finished my work. Too many interruptions make the animals nervous."

"You can count on me, Señor Doctor."

Lucky Sam laughed silently as he hurried down the dark passageway. The flatfoot had actually saluted him! Wait until he told Don Pepe. The empresario had drawn a small map, detailing the subterranean mysteries of the arena, and Lucky Sam continued past the stabled horses to the first of several holding pens located behind the toril gate. On the side of each pen was a chalked number, and the Chinese inventor stopped at #119. Using a length of board to prod the animal's rump, he urged the bull forward into the stanchions and locked his head in place.

Lucky Sam whistled a medley from "La Traviata" as he took off his jacket and rolled up his sleeves. In the doctor's bag he found a canvas apron, which he tied about his waist. Next, he laid out the instruments in a neat, stainless-steel row: syringe, scalpel, bone drill, curved suturing needle, surgical clamps and hemostats. The last item out of the bag was a transistorized stimulator/radio receiver no larger than the dial of a wristwatch, and bristling with fine wires. Lucky Sam placed it carefully in line with the other tools. Behind him in the pen, bull #119 was urinating. The fastidious Oriental mechanical wizard took a step backward to keep his socks from getting splattered.

While the empresario Don Pepe caroused with his cronies in the other room, Carlos Carretera, looking rested after four nights in jail, stood by the window, gazing down at the rented Hispano-Suiza parked in front of the hotel. He was deeply into the role of el Chicote, aspirant matador, with a tendency to pose near any handy reflection. Moving from the window glass to the mirror over the dresser, Carlos studied his image and straightened his shoulders.

His satin pants were nicely mended, although he noticed a run in one of his pink stockings. The glittering gold-embroidered jacket lay carefully folded on the bed; his narrow tie hung from the top of the mirror. Soon he would finish dressing, but first, in lacy shirt sleeves and suspenders, el Chicote got down on his knees before the plaster Virgin on the dresser. This was a good pose: flickering votive candle in one hand, his shirt open at the throat, a tousled forelock tumbling as he bent his head in prayer. "Our nada who art in nada, nada be thy name. . . ."

The lime-green Maserati spun to a stop behind the main hacienda and a pursuing cloud of chalk-colored dust threatened to envelop everyone in the courtyard. Paco Machismo peered through the billowing grit and peeled off his perforated pigskin driving gloves. Safety-belted into the bucket seat beside him, Mercy Malone was waving at Abe Wasserman and Marty Farb, unmistakable in their sunglasses and boldly patterned dashikis. A girl doesn't get that many chances to wave at Hollywood producers, and Mercy was giving it her all.

"Bienvenido, Paco," the Conde de San Conejo called, advancing with open arms into the settling dust. "My house is your house."

Paco Machismo pulled himself from the low-slung automobile and embraced the elderly count. "It is an honor, your Lordship."

"Howdy, partner," Abe Wasserman said, extending his hand for a hearty shake. Marty Farb was right behind with a big smile.

Paco waved Mercy over and introduced her to the Conde de San Conejo.

"It is always an honor to have so beautiful a visitor," the Count said, bending to kiss her hand.

"Amen!" Abe Wasserman lifted his highball glass in salute.

"Where's Alfredo?" Paco asked. "I thought he would be here today."

"This boy never goes anywhere without his manager," Marty Farb said. "Pretty smart."

"Don't worry, Paco." The venerable count patted the young matador on the back. "Alfredo went to the house to get you both a drink. I have a case of Pepsi on ice in honor of your visit. We were on our way to have a look at the . . . animal when we heard your car approaching."

"Ah, yes, the animal, where do you keep it?"

"In a small arena behind the calfing sheds; the first two days it ran free in the marsh but that was too dangerous. Are you anxious to see it or shall we wait until after lunch?"

"I know the lunch will be excellent, Excellency, but it is not fine food which brings me here today."

"Then by all means, let's satisfy your curiosity."

"Wait till you get a load of this critter, Paco," Abe Wasserman said. "It's antediluvian."

El número uno answered with a finger snap and a swagger. "I don't care what its politics are, I want to know if it will charge straight."

The Conde de San Conejo led his guests across the farmyard, past monumental stone barns and granaries, to a wooden grandstand overlooking a circular arena. Paco was reminded of provincial towns where amateur corridas were held annually on the feast day of the local patron saint.

"We use this to amuse our visitors, caping calves and fighting cows," the old count said. "Today it would be a good place for a safari."

"Jesus and Mary protect you, Paco," wailed Mercy Malone. "Just look at the size of that bugger."

Abe Wasserman was smiling. "That baby weighs close to two tons and is meaner than Primo Carnera with a hangover."

Stolid as a bulldozer, the rhinoceros grazed on a scattered hay bale in the center of the arena, not bothering to raise his massive armor-plated head or acknowledge the presence of his excited admirers.

"Okay, matador," Marty Farb said. "That's no Elsie the Borden cow out there; don't it make you want to say your rosary real quick?"

Paco Machismo curled his upper lip with disdain, the look that made the conquistadors famous. "It only has one horn," he sneered. "The odds are already in my favor."

El Camión had a headache. The fighting bull waited in his dark pen, the first fierce flashes strobing out of the icy numbness between his horns. Even for an animal by nature ill-tempered, el Camión's mood was exceptionally

65

foul. Many centuries of inbred genetic viciousness conspired to produce this wrathful monster. All his systems were Go.

Hatred comes naturally to a fighting bull, but el Camión's black rage was something altogether new. As the anesthetic wore off, the bull felt a strange presence between his horns. Shaking his head didn't dislodge it and el Camión was unable to rub the spot against the side of the pen because of his wide, curving horns. Whatever this itching thing was, the two-legged had caused it. Fighting bull #119 stood very still in the darkness, remembering the pink ballooning of intestines that follows a horn thrust. Once, on the ranch, el Camión had disemboweled a horse. A two-legged would split open even more easily.

At the first fandango peal of the trumpet, Esmeralda Fabada entered the bullring on the arm of an American sailor. They had expensive front-row seats in the barrera section and pushed their way along the crowded aisle as the band began to play "La Virgen de la Macarena" at the start of the bullfighter's paseo.

Three matadors led the procession, sunlight brilliant on their trajes de luces, their left arms wrapped in the ceremonial capes. They walked with an easy, fluid swagger, and behind them in orderly rows marched the cuadrillas of banderilleros, mounted picadors, and the monosabios in red shirts, leading the mule teams which remove the dead bulls.

Esmeralda thrilled at the glittering sight of these brave toreros. Today she would share their glory. At the first opportunity it was over the rail and into the arena. She ignored the bosun's mate shoving peanuts into his pink face at her side and tapped her heelless slippers impatiently in time with the music.

. . .

El Chicote was a very nervous matador. He waited behind the barrera and watched the first two bulls of the afternoon go to their deaths with a minimum of difficulty. The second kill was quite elegant and stylish and, in spite of a poor showing with the muleta, the jubilant torero was awarded an ear and a tour of the ring. As he paraded past el Chicote, clutching his bloody trophy, the rival matador winked and called out over the cheering, "You're next, Aviator, better strap on your wings."

"Don't listen to that shit, Carlos," his manager whispered. The empresario felt the boy trembling when he took hold of his arm. "There's nothing to worry about; I've made certain arrangements." On the contrary, there was everything to worry about; Lucky Sam Wo had yet to appear or send any sort of message and Don Pepe was worried sick.

"Tell me again how big he is, Don Pepe." The quaver in el Chicote's voice was every bit as haunting as a flamenco singer's keening.

"He's a big one all right, but never mind his size, it's all taken care of. You're going to look good out there."

"But what should I do? How should I handle him?"

Don Pepe was about to advise caution when he saw Sam Wo come into the arena. The Chinaman hurried down the concrete steps. For the first time that afternoon, Don Pepe permitted himself a small smile. "Why, Carlos, handle him bravely," he said. "Be bold. Take chances. No harm will come to you, I promise. In fact, why not try something showy? Plant yourself on your knees before the toril gate and pass the bull with a cambio de rodillas on his charge into the ring."

"But . . . Don Pepe, that would be suicide."

"Nonsense, it's fixed, I tell you. Now go on out there, you're up. And remember: on your knees, it's a crowd-pleaser."

Don Pepe watched el Chicote stride into the bullring. His legs were shaking badly but on his knees the kid would be a sensation in there today.

"Pepe! Pepe!"

The empresario turned at the sound of his friend's voice. "Hurry, Pepe," the Chinaman called.

"What's the matter, amigo? What made you so late?" Don Pepe grinned in anticipation of Chicote's triumph.

"Pepe, come over here. We're in trouble."

"Something go wrong with the operation?" The empresario's smile faded.

"No, the operation went fine."

"What is it then?"

"The suitcase—"

"What suitcase?"

"The suitcase with the control system; on the way over here I got jumped by a pair of strong-arm boys. They stole it, Pepe; they stole the suitcase!"

"Isn't there something you can do?"

"Not without the controls. The bull will act normal until the 'stimuceiver' is turned on."

"Poor Carlos, I've signed his death warrant." The empresario stared dolefully at the bullring as el Chicote lowered himself to his knees in the sand.

"Listen, Pepe," Lucky Sam said, "I put McHaggis on this. If anyone can find the thieves, he can. He's got the word out among those who buy stolen goods. The suitcase will turn up, you'll see."

But Don Pepe was no longer listening. Anticipatory mourner's tears welled in his bloodshot eyes.

• • •

Esmeralda Fabada watched eagerly as the novillero, el Chicote, walked the length of the arena, trembling like the leaves of a poplar. The matador's fear telegraphed across the arena and all the knowledgeable customers in the cheap seats hooted with derision. This Chicote was the answer to Esmeralda's prayers. She was waiting for a clumsy matador, and a provident fate had provided the Aviator. It was said that not once in his career had he finished a corrida on his feet. When the novillero dropped to his knees less than ten varas from the toril gate, Esmeralda knew she would soon get her chance.

The trumpet called and the toril gate swung open. There was a long moment when time itself seemed to hold its breath; then, *boom*, the very darkness of the shadowy passageway congealed, and like a chunk of midnight, a tremendous black bull thundered out of the bowels of the stadium. The huge animal never slowed his initial charge across the arena. El Chicote, kneeling directly in his path, made an absurd flapping motion with the cape and was gathered up in a pitchfork toss of those wide, gleaming horns and flung like a rag doll high into the air, arms and legs akimbo. As the novillero nose-dived into the sand, the fighting bull, el Camión, rammed the barrera on the opposite side of the ring, splintering the red-painted boards and sending peons and sword-handlers diving for cover.

No one dared to make the quite. El Chicote staggered to his feet and was run over like a drunk lurching in front of a taxicab. The fighting bull trampled the unfortunate matador and continued his circuit of the arena. The other matadors ducked back behind the barrera to safety as the huge bull came snorting by. El Chicote lay sprawled like a sack of dirty laundry, alone in the ring. It was the chance of a lifetime.

Esmeralda stood on the railing and leaped over the

heads of sword-handlers and plainclothes police into the arena. Her pleated red skirt opened like the petals of a poppy as the crowd roared approval. The girl sprang to her feet and ran toward the circling bull, pausing once to pirouette with her hands above her head. At the sight of her beautiful smiling face the crowd went berserk.

Esmeralda Fabada stopped at the exact center of the bullring in that terrain which is called medias. She struck a dancer's pose and clapped her hands twice above her head. Over by the toril gate, the black, heavy-necked bull turned and looked. As he lowered his head for the charge, Esmeralda unbuttoned her pleated skirt and removed it with a flourish.

A roar burst from the crowd like a volcano erupting. The sight of a nearly naked young woman standing alone and vulnerable in the path of a charging bull awoke passions long forgotten. Not since the days of ancient Crete, when bare-breasted maidens performed acrobatics with wild aurochs, vaulting the high, curving horns, had such a cry been heard in any arena.

The crowd's howl built in volume as the gap between bull and girl closed. There was a moment of fusion, a merging of the hulking black animal and the slender pale-white body into a single image, divided by the fluid, float-ing swirl of red skirt. No ballet could boast a more dramatic *pas de deux*. Esmeralda passed the bull with a graceful veronica and the inarticulate uproar formed a single word: *"Olé!"*

The girl's control was perfect and the crowd responded to her every move, answering each successful pass with an enthusiastic "Olé." Esmeralda wore the tails of her blouse tied up under her breasts, leaving her midriff bare, and during a thrillingly executed pachanga, the bull's horn tip traced a thin red line as fine as a thorn scratch across the lipstick letters printed on her milk-white tummy.

Completing the interlinked sequence of passes with a reverse zarzuela, Esmeralda turned to acknowledge the applause, her right hand high in a victor's salute. The ovation continued even as four policemen darted into the arena to grab the unsuspecting girl. A torrent of beer bottles and seat cushions emphasized the crowd's displeasure as the forces of the law hustled the struggling espontánea back behind the barrera. A thousand voices in unison chanted the name they had grown to love:

"Fabalita . . .

FABALITA . . .

FABALITA!"

El Camión was confused. He backed into his querencia by the toril gate to think things over. His enemies the two-leggeds were everywhere in the ring. The one with the long mane, who continued to fool him with the cloth even though he knew it was a trick, was held by as many as four. The other, with the shining gold scales, was also being carried; a pair of two-leggeds dressed in white picked him off the sand and ran, stumbling, back behind the barrera. El Camión had the arena to himself.

The bull sniffed the blood drying on his flank, licking upward toward the beribboned divisa harpooned into the erect hump of muscle rising behind his neck. Another indignity suffered on account of enemies too cowardly to face his wrath. El Camión lifted his head and squinted nearsightedly at the howling spectators, arranged in tiers above him. A herd of two-leggeds reaching to the sky. He wanted to annihilate them all.

• • •

The first to note the intention of the bull's charge was an American tourist focusing his Hasselblad from the third row of the shaded section. The maddened animal grew larger and larger through the lenses until the viewfinder was filled with blackness and the astonished autoparts manufacturer looked up to see el Camión hurtling over the barrera like a steeplechaser.

With the ease of Zeus on an adulterous, taurine foray, the fighting bull cleared the callejón, that narrow passage between the barrera wall and the first row of seats, and landed, kicking and slashing, in the grandstand. Those privileged with barrera seats were the first to be tossed backward into the arena. One screaming woman was impaled where she sat, right through the bag of oranges resting in her lap.

Hundreds of terrified spectators scrambled for cover as el Camión started up the aisle. A policeman standing five steps above fired two shots; the first pierced the bull's ear and struck the American with the Hasselblad over the left eye; the second went wild, straight up into the cloudless sky in a mad race for heaven with the soul of the unsuccessful marksman.

Wicked horns wet with blood, el Camión pursued the panicking crowd down the long exit tunnel, spearing the tardy at random and pausing near the main entrance to overturn a ticket booth. Out in the street it was pure pandemonium. Fleeing spectators stampeded across four lanes of afternoon traffic, turning the crowded avenue into an instant demolition derby. The bull stood for a moment and observed the carnage, enjoying the sweet sight of so many two-leggeds at the mercy of this mechanized chaos. He bellowed with pleasure, took a leisurely piss and chased a woman wheeling a perambulator down the tree-lined boulevard.

. . .

El Chicote's eyes were bright with morphine. The wounded novillero lay on the table in the bullring infirmary and smiled. He counted these emergency-room moments among the happiest of his life. There were always a few curious onlookers, and having an audience made it seem dramatic. He was the star of the show.

While the surgeons cleaned and stitched a nine-inch cornada in el Chicote's thigh, the empresario read for a second time the note just delivered by messenger service. It was from McHaggis: "Pepe—I have the suitcase. P. Castaño, 48 Calle Calderón, second floor front. Castaño claims he paid 3000 pesetas but I doubt it. I'll wait here until you come or I hear otherwise.—Mac."

"Luck returns to me," Sam Wo said, reading over Don Pepe's shoulder. "For a while I was beginning to doubt my sobriquet."

"Luck? Three thousand pesetas is not luck; three thousand pesetas is extortion."

"Pepe, be reasonable, it would cost five thousand pesetas to have the true price beaten out of this pawnbroker."

"Even if he wanted fifty céntimos it would be too much." Don Pepe pointed to the operating table. "Look at poor Carlos and tell me about my luck. Let them keep the suitcase. It's too late to do me any good."

"But it's not too late for you to go to jail again, old man." Sam Wo assumed a sinister Fu Manchu inscrutability. "The bull is loose in the streets; sooner or later it will be shot. When the cops find the wires in his head they'll make it the case of the remote-controlled bull. You and I will take the rap if someone is killed, unless . . ."

"Unless?" The empresario was all ears.

"Unless we get to the animal first, and for that we need

the control panel to immobilize him. The garrotte is not so pretty around your throat as that lavender necktie, my friend; is three thousand pesetas too high a price to pay for your life?"

"Paco, I don't care how much they're paying you, it can't be worth it." Mercy Malone slouched on the contoured leather seat and studied the bullfighter's stern profile. "All the money in the world isn't enough for getting in the ring with that monster."

El número uno downshifted as they came up behind a slow-moving delivery truck. "Money I make by accident," he snarled. "Rooting is for pigs."

"Then what do you do it for, kicks?"

"For the feeling it gives me, yes. There is nothing else in the world like that feeling, my darling, not even making love to you."

"You really get your rocks off out there in the ring, right, Paco? Those bulls are pretty sexy, I've got to admit."

"I used to fight three times a day as a novillero. That was the best summer of my life; five of us in a rented Fiat, driving from one country feria to another all through the provinces. I would give all the money in the world to taste those first sweet thrills once again."

Mercy rolled a candy-covered anise seed around the inside of her mouth. "If you get off on danger, I guess the rhino is going to be the biggest thrill of all."

"It is an interesting challenge." El número uno yawned.

"Am I?"

"Are you what?"

"An interesting challenge?"

Paco Machismo smiled. "I think you are jealous of the rhinoceros."

At that moment, a black fighting bull with the bent wheel of a baby carriage dangling from one horn rounded the corner ahead of them and galloped down a side street.

"Jesus, Mary and Joseph!" Mercy cried.

Paco turned hard on the wheel and urged the sleek Maserati past the delivery truck in pursuit. Halfway down the block, the fighting bull stopped, distracted by a display in the window of a dress shop. As Paco pulled over to the curb, the rampaging animal charged through a hailstorm of shattering plate glass and attacked the frozen figures of three mannequins costumed in white satin bridal gowns.

"Did you hear that?" the policeman sitting by the window asked the driver. He turned up the volume on the two-way radio but the dispatcher had finished and only the uneven crackle of static was amplified. "Did you hear what he just said?"

"No," the driver said. "I missed it."

"It's the bull; the big one, he's running wild in the streets. He must have jumped the barrera. I tell you, hombre, that one is very much of a bull."

"Do you remember his name?"

"No, but he was some bull all right."

"Ask the girl, maybe she knows."

The policeman slid back the metal hatch and rapped on the wire grille covering the opening into the rear of the van. "Hey, chiquita," he called. "Hey, you still in there?"

"No. I've gone to Paris for *le weekend*." The girl sat in the dark with two older women, prostitutes picked up for soliciting among the ticket lines outside the Plaza de Toros, and it was hard to tell which of them had spoken.

"I'm talking to you, Fabalita, not them other two tarts. Listen, kid, I saw you in the ring today and you got a pair

75

of balls any man'd be proud to have. What you did took true cojones. That bull was a mountain, all right. My partner was wondering if you remembered his name."

"Camión," the girl said.

"That's right, el Camión; only he was bigger than any truck. That was the biggest bull I've ever seen."

"It's not size that counts," one of the prostitutes hooted. Her friend at her side giggled loudly.

"Fabalita, you deserve better company than these mattress mechanics." The policeman sounded genuinely sorrowful. "Might make you feel better to know that el Camión is free. He jumped the barrera and is roaming around somewhere in the city."

The prostitutes snickered. "Why aren't you cops out chasing the bull instead of picking on innocent women like us?"

"Innocent, my ass! You broads weren't innocent on your confirmation day." The policeman closed the metal hatch. "Can you believe that pair of putas?" he asked his partner. "The next thing they'll be telling us they're nuns."

Paco Machismo bolted from the crouching automobile and jumped through the shattered show window into the shop. Dismembered mannequins lay strewn about like war victims. The bull raged in the back by the dressing rooms, his head entangled in a beribboned hoopskirt. Several excited customers, in varying stages of undress, pressed against the walls, shrieking.

El número uno pulled off his tailored silk jacket and hurried down the central aisle. "Don't move, ladies," he commanded. "Everyone keep still until I distract the bull. When he is occupied with me, run for the street."

The hoopskirt hung in shreds from the gleaming upturned horns and Paco Machismo looked straight into the bull's staring red eye as he edged closer along the side of a glass-topped display counter. "Huh, toro," he grunted, stamping his size six foot. The bull lowered his head and charged. "Run, ladies!" Paco Machismo called, circling his short silk jacket about his waist, a rebolera which turned the bull so sharply that the great animal skidded to its knees on the slick terrazzo floor.

Machismo backed away, flapping his jacket in the bull's face to hold his attention while the women made their escape. Dancing on his toes, the skillful matador lured the bull to the back of the shop and began a bold and seldom-seen pachuco. As the bull charged past, the sleeve of the jacket caught on a horn tip and the makeshift cape was jerked from el número uno's hands.

Paco Machismo was disarmed. In the bullring this would be considered a dishonor and he might expect some jeering from the crowd, but at least there was always a mono nearby to hand him a fresh muleta from behind the barrera. Alone in the dress shop he was on his own, backed into a corner with no way out.

Don Pepe held a gloved finger to the doorbell and waited; the angry buzz inside was muffled but insistent, like a hornet trapped under a water glass. Behind him in the shadows of the dusty hallway lurked Lucky Sam Wo. Presently, footsteps were heard within the apartment. A small square of light opened in the center of the door, framing a single curious eye.

"Is this Castaño?" Don Pepe asked.

"Sí, and who are you?"

"McHaggis sent for me."

"Who's that with you?"

"A friend. Stop playing games and let us in."

The bolt was drawn and the door opened just wide

enough to permit the empresario and the Chinese inventor a furtive entrance. They followed the stoop-shouldered Castaño through a series of dark rooms to the kitchen. McHaggis stood by the stove, drinking coffee. The suitcase was on the table.

"Hello, Mac," Don Pepe said. "Did you tell this blood-sucker that I won't go higher than fifteen hundred pesetas?"

"Be reasonable," Castaño squeaked. "I paid three thousand for the item. It's only fair that I get my investment back."

"Who would pay three thousand pesetas for an old suitcase?"

"Look inside, it's full of electronical stuff. The parts alone are worth money." Castaño polished his rimless spectacles with the end of his necktie. "I thought this was supposed to be your suitcase."

Don Pepe pulled out his billfold and extracted a number of limp banknotes. "It belongs to my friend," he said. "This is a favor for him. Next time I won't be so generous."

Castaño pocketed the money. "It's always a pleasure to do business with gentlemen," he said.

Lucky Sam Wo stepped to the table and unfastened the latches on the suitcase. "This is one investment you'll never regret, Pepe."

The empresario shrugged. "So, there's going to be a small corrida next week in Sueño de Duende. I'll book Carlos for the fight and reimburse myself out of what he earns."

"But think about his leg, Pepe," the Chinaman said, opening the suitcase lid. "He didn't cut himself shaving."

"The leg will heal."

"You can be a hard man, Pepe." Sam Wo checked the

radio equipment nestled inside the suitcase, expertly re-connecting a pair of loose wires.

"Not hard, my friend," Don Pepe said, leaning forward to flip a small silver toggle switch that the smiling Oriental indicated with his pocket screwdriver. "Not hard. Only practical."

Mercy Malone watched four screaming lingerie-clad women flee the dress salon and run off down the street. There was a sound of crashing glass inside and three more frantic ladies came running out. "These must be the shop-girls," Mercy decided. "They've all got their clothes on. Very considerate to let the customers go first."

Still, there was nothing at all considerate about not a single one sticking around to see what happened to poor Paco, and him risking his life for them, too. This made Mercy's Celtic temper rise and she stormed across the sidewalk and into the store, determined to stand fast in the face of danger. No daughter of County Cork would be seen scampering down the avenue in her undies on account of recalcitrant cattle.

In spite of her bold entrance, Mercy was unprepared for the sight of Paco backed against the wall defenseless, and the bull, blacker than a fiend from hell itself, poised for the final charge. "Oh, he's a dead man surely," she cried, and indeed, he looked like a cadaver with the color drained from his suntanned face, although no martyr before a firing squad ever stood any straighter.

Mercy covered her eyes with her hands when the bull started running, but she couldn't resist opening her fingers a crack for one last peek. This was how she would always remember Paco—serene and brave, a faint smile lingering on his pale lips. "Adios," she whispered.

Suddenly, in mid-stride, the huge creature lurched to a

stumbling stop less than ten feet from where Paco stood. All of the bull's bunched muscles sagged and the animal seemed to settle and shrink as if someone had pulled the plug and was letting out the air. Paco blinked in disbelief.

For several seconds, no one moved; then Paco took a first tentative step and when that got no reaction from the bull he was emboldened to try another, and soon he was safely off to one side behind an overturned showcase. The bull continued to stare straight ahead.

"What happened, Paco?" Mercy called from the doorway.

"I don't know. Es peculiar." The matador tried clapping his hands, and still the bull didn't so much as turn his head.

"It's a miracle, that's what it is."

Satisfied the bull was not going to move, Paco Machismo hunted through the wreckage until he found four leather belts to hobble the big animal's legs. "If he changes his mind, those should hold him."

"A bloomin' miracle, there's no other word for it." Mercy reached out a cautious hand and patted the gleaming black flank. "Paco, what's going to happen to the bull?"

"He'll go to the slaughterhouse, they can't risk using him in the ring any more."

"But that doesn't seem fair." Mercy slid her hand over the glossy hide. "This bull is special, Paco; I mean, he could have killed you."

"That is not so especial. Many bulls have had that opportunity."

"No, I'm talking about the way he just stopped, as if God Himself reached out and took him by the tail. You can't let this miraculous creature end up as a pile of hamburger. Paco, why don't you buy him?"

Paco Machismo laughed. "I don't want him. I see enough of them in the corrida. In any case, what would I do with a fighting bull?"

"You could keep it at your country place. How much is it worth, anyway?" Mercy traced her manicured fingertips over the weltlike numerals branded on the bull's rump.

"Right now he's only worth the price of beef; so much a kilo, depending on the market."

"In that case, I'll buy him myself. A souvenir of my trip to Spain."

El Camión was glassy-eyed. Not since his days as a calf gamboling in the new spring clover had he experienced such innocent bliss. His black heart no longer raged with a compulsion to destroy. A feeling of peace and well-being held him transfixed.

Warm, happy thoughts flooded his dim taurine consciousness: he remembered the soft lapping of his mother's tongue and the security of her bountiful udders. He felt the calm presence of the herd everywhere around him. Even when the two-legged bound his feet with leather straps, el Camión was undisturbed. The fighting bull stared unblinking into the middle distance, mindlessly chewing an imaginary cud.

martes

IN THE MORNING, the posters were up all over town, two sizes larger than the average bullfight cartel, but in the same traditional style:

PLAZA DE TOROS MUNICIPAL
DOMINGO 30 DE AGOSTO
GRANDIOSA CORRIDA
For the First Time in History
PACO MACHISMO
El Número Uno—the Bravest Among the Brave
Will Fight to the Death in the Spanish Fashion
UN RINOCERONTE
Captured Wild in Africa
A Spectacle Never Before Seen on Earth
RESERVE YOUR TICKETS PRONTO

Wherever it had been posted—on the sides of buildings, against barroom walls, in multiples over the curving exteriors of outdoor public urinals—crowds gathered to stare. Even the illiterate were attracted by the picture: a waiting matador and his magenta-and-yellow cape mere dabs of color dwarfed by the looming gray monster. Some of the onlookers gaped in silence. Others, especially those gathered in taverns and bodegas, waved their arms and raised their voices.

By noon, most of the reserved seats in the shade were sold out and the lines in front of the general-admission ticket windows stretched for blocks. It was the biggest thing to hit the city since the Inquisition provided free public entertainment in the Plaza Mayor.

Across the street from the rear of the woman's prison the novillero, el Chicote, leaned against a lamppost, keeping his weight off his bad leg. He stared compassionately at the somber brick walls and barred windows. It was less than a week since he too had been a prisoner and the distinction between inside and outside was one he was able to appreciate.

Shortly after midday, a black, bolt-studded iron door swung open and a dark-haired girl wearing a pleated red skirt stepped blinking into the sunlight. She was handed a small parcel by a guard standing inside and the solid door swung closed. Chicote limped in pursuit, catching the girl before she reached the corner. "They always bring you in through the front door and let you out at the back," he said. "I know, I've been inside myself."

The girl regarded him coldly. "Are you proud of that?" she asked. "It requires no great talent to go to jail."

The novillero bowed and extended his hand. "My name is Carlos Carretera. I want to thank you for saving my life." The girl ignored his outstretched hand. Her gaze was as expressionless as a traffic light. "In the ring, I'm called 'el Chicote'," Carlos continued. "That big bull,

Camión, nearly finished me on Sunday. If it hadn't been for you, I'd be a dead man today."

"Your life means nothing to me. What I did was for myself only. Now, if you will excuse me, señor—"

"Wait! You don't understand. No one else had the courage to make the quite with that bull. I don't care what your motives were, you saved my life and I'm grateful. I want you to accept my sincere gratitude."

"All right, I accept it. If that satisfies you, may I go?"

"First, tell me your name. All I know is that they call you 'la Fabalita.'"

"Fabalita is good enough."

"Fine, bueno, let it be Fabalita then. Listen, I know the slop you're fed in the carcel; why don't you let me take you to a good restaurant for a proper meal?"

La Fabalita scrutinized his threadbare suit. "And how will you settle your account—by having me scrub the floor?"

"No, I have money. My manager gave me a quarter of a lottery ticket that was a winner. Look." Carlos pulled a handful of crumpled pesetas from his pocket. "See, there's enough here for a suckling pig."

"Cochinillo," the girl whispered fondly.

"Why not? I have money, you saved my life; isn't that reason enough for a feast?"

The white mouse sat up on his hindquarters in the aromatic nest of cedar shavings and drank a single drop of water from the inverted bottle attached to the side of the cage. Whiskers trembling, the albino rejoined one of his innumerable cousins for a last run on the wheel as Doña Carlota Madrigal reached in and seized him by the tail with a gloved hand.

Señora Madrigal carried the dangling rodent at arm's

length. She wore her gardening gloves not for protection—the docile, quivering creatures never struggled or bit—but because she couldn't stand to touch the naked tails. Mice were disgusting animals; no matter if their white fur was as sterile as the laboratories for which they were bred, the señora suspected them of harboring fleas and mites.

Along the far wall of the room where Carlota Madrigal raised her desert plants and cacti a series of glass cases housed her son's collection of lizards and snakes native to arid regions. The largest of these contained a half-dozen sand-colored sidewinder rattlesnakes. The señora marched straight up to this case, opened the screened cover and dropped in the mouse.

Bending down, she stared through the glass at the miniature desert environment inside. The sidewinders undulated through the sand, weaving their sinuous track between the night-blooming cereus. The blunt horns standing over their hooded yellow eyes gave these snakes a diabolical look. The eyes of the mouse were pink pinheads, innocent of everything, including intelligence, and the tiny warm-blooded mammal sat very still as the cold presence of the serpent slid past.

"Read any good news lately, Pepe?" grunted Andrew McHaggis, dusting a spot on the park bench next to the empresario. The elderly Scotsman opened a small paper bag full of breadcrumbs and soon had a flock of pigeons bobbing at his feet.

Don Pepe continued to turn pages, scanning headlines and muttering to himself. "Not a word . . . not a single word . . . nothing, nada . . . not even in the back pages." He crumpled the newspaper in his lap. "Mac, I've been over the morning edition three times and there's nothing. Yesterday they had nearly a page, photographs and everything; today, zero."

"Relax, Pepe, what you don't see can't hurt you."

"I suppose you're trying to tell me that you had no luck either."

"Well, I haven't found the bull, but I managed to uncover one or two interesting things." McHaggis scattered a final handful of crumbs over the heads of the murmuring birds. "First I checked with my sources at police headquarters, and as far as anyone there knows, the animal is still alive. They delivered it to the contractor at the stockyards, but today's cattle invoice showed no record of its being slaughtered. I checked the corrals but there were only steers, no fighting bulls."

"But that's impossible, a bull can't just disappear from the stockyards."

McHaggis dusted the crumbs from his hands and lit his briar pipe. "The contractor wouldn't tell me anything, but I loosened the tongue of one of the yardmen with a few shots of brandy and he said that a woman driving a white convertible and pulling a horse trailer came the night before and that he and two others loaded the bull onto the trailer and she took it away. Normally I wouldn't have believed him, a fighting bull in a horse trailer sounds absurd. But it matches something I learned from the cops; the papers claimed Machismo subdued a wild bull, but according to all I've heard, the animal was as gentle as a newborn babe. What did you dope it with, Pepe?"

"Never mind that now." Don Pepe huffed to his feet. "What about Paco Machismo? Perhaps he bought the bull?"

"I thought of that, too, but if he did, he's not keeping it at his finca. I sent someone out to check this morning."

"You do good work, Mac. Come, let me buy you a

drink. When you find that bull it'll be worth a whole bottle."

Mercy Malone used the tack-room entrance when visiting the stables of the exclusive Francisco Cortina Riding Academy; that way she avoided the jodhpur set gathered for a stirrup cup in the foyer. All the grooms and trainers were in love with her. They knew she was Paco Machismo's girl and competed with each other to see who could do her the most favors. El Camión's stall was kept well scrubbed and clean straw always covered the floor.

Mercy waved to the boys hosing a lathered mount down after a ride. The stable boys grinned awkwardly and blew her kisses. A pity there wasn't a cute one in the lot. Considering her mood today, Mercy would gladly have screwed anyone in the barn, if only to get even with Paco for being such a prick about letting her keep the bull out at his finca. "Isn't it enough that I keep you around?" the man had said. "Must I house your livestock as well?" The arrogant bastard!

El Camión stood placidly in his stall. Mercy leaned against the fragrant alfalfa-filled manger and admired his massive sleekness. The fighting bull's weight was all forward; his shoulders bunched with muscle. A humped, brawny crest rose behind his neck and tapered down to the middle of his back. His hindquarters were as graceful and delicate as a pony's.

Mercy rubbed her hands against his pelt, kneading the fluid muscles with her slender fingers. "The Japs massage their beef, I've read," she said to the bull. "How do you like this treatment? You've got your own private geisha girl now."

El Camión stared blankly ahead, his head lowered as Mercy rubbed and massaged him from one end to the other. The Irish girl sang as she labored over the bull's flanks. The big animal's hide was smooth and warm; the tuft of hair at the end of his tail as fine as any silk on earth. And when Mercy saw the heavy, hanging scrotum she sucked in her breath. She cupped the weighty balls in both her hands, marveling at their size and softness. Mercy longed to see him erect but the mighty member remained sheathed in spite of the girl's ardent stroking. "Ah me," she sighed. "Of all the bulls in the world, I had to find a queer."

"I want to thank you gentlemen for granting me this interview." Lucky Sam Wo spoke impeccable Oxford English as he paced the Moroccan rug in the hotel suite of Toro Productions. "I appreciate how busy you must be."

"Time is money," Abe Wasserman said, lighting a ten-dollar Havana cigar.

"Then, by all means, let us proceed without further delay. Have you a television?"

"Inna corner." Marty Farb pointed with his thumb like a hitchiker.

"I have a short presentation." Lucky Sam carried his briefcase-sized video tape-recorder over and plugged it into the TV set. "It runs under ten minutes. I knew the moment I saw your poster that you gentlemen were innovators, men with imagination. Well, I'll let the tape speak for itself." Lucky Sam placed a cassette in the machine and adjusted the picture and sound. On the screen, slightly out of focus, his mechanical bull pawed the workshop floor.

"What's a bull doing in a warehouse?" Marty Farb demanded.

"Shhh! Listen," Abe Wasserman said. "You might learn something."

The image on the screen showed an early trial run before the taxidermist's upholstery job. All of the robot's cogs and pistons were visible as it charged across an open field. Lucky Sam's narration stressed his theory of the deathless bullfight and its potential with American audiences. In a demonstration of strength, the mechanical animal was shown overturning a Volkswagen microbus. The brief tape ended with a shot of the robot wandering undetected through a browsing herd of three-year-old fighting bulls.

"Quite a contraption you got there," Abe Wasserman said as the screen went blank.

"It can be operated either by remote control or on automatic," the Chinese inventor explained. "This makes transportation no problem. You drive it like a car."

"Very impressive," Marty Farb grunted. "Only one question: What's all this got to do with us?"

"Ah, yes, of course, I was hoping we could make a deal. I propose to offer the use of my creation for your program, free of charge, as a preliminary spectacle before the main event."

"What's in this deal for you, professor, if you don't want any money?" Abe Wasserman asked.

"I am interested in the publicity. Most bullfight promoters are too tradition-bound to take a chance. You would give me the opportunity to demonstrate my machine to the public; in return, I would give you a free . . . curtain raiser, I believe it's called."

"I tell you what, prof," Abe said. "I don't usually do business on the spur of the moment like this, but I'll take you up on your offer on one condition: you got to supply your own matador. I know all about those traditions you mentioned. Finding a bullfighter to take on our rhino was like pulling teeth. You come up with a toreador willing to fight a robot and I'll even pay for the extra posters; now how's that for a deal?"

Paco Machismo disliked the zoo. It was hot and noisy. Phalanxes of uniformed schoolchildren trooped everywhere, herded by sharp-voiced nuns. The smells, unlike the sweetness of the barnyard, were an acrid blend of musk and urine. The sight of so many caged animals made him unhappy.

Paco stood for a while outside the tiger's cage, anonymous behind his dark glasses, a helium-filled balloon thrust upon him by a balloon-selling extortionist clutched in one hand. The big cat was fat and healthy. His coat gleamed in the sunlight. He paced relentlessly back and forth the length of the narrow cell, razor claws useless within his padded feet. The sympathy Paco Machismo felt for the tiger was modified by disgust. "Better to starve in freedom than grow fat in a cage," he thought, continuing on through the crowd. This was his first trip to the zoo and he was lost. Fear of recognition prevented him from asking directions, but at last, over by the elefantes, he found what he was looking for.

The rhinoceros compound was a small island of packed sand enclosed by a dry moat. Two of the surly plated beasts stood swaying from foot to foot beside a pile of hay. Numbers of small birds hopped along their backs, picking ticks from the thick, cracked skin. One even ventured within a rhino's ear and the huge, shuffling creature merely blinked at the intrusion. Paco Machismo leaned against a surrounding iron fence and tossed a bagful of peanuts into the enclosure. As the uneven-toed mammals lumbered forward to investigate, el número uno focused his Polaroid camera, intent on their every move.

· · ·

All that remained of the roast suckling pig was his apple-clenching grin. The rest of the animal, from snout to curling tail, was reduced to a disorganized pile of bones. Every morsel of pig, including the singed tips of his pointed ears, had been devoured. Esmeralda sucked her greasy fingers and smiled contentedly. "Sabroso," she sighed.

Carlos Carretera picked his teeth and sipped a glass of Valdepeñas. "Not bad; I am pleased that you enjoyed yourself."

"It was delicious."

"Bueno." El Chicote clapped his hands for the waiter and ordered coffee. Bending like a conspirator over the pig bones he whispered, "Listen, I have a proposition to make you."

Esmeralda's smile changed ever so slightly from a string of pearls to a strand of barbed wire. "Naturally," she said, "first the dinner, then the proposition; that's the usual procedure, is it not?"

"No, no, you misunderstand me," el Chicote stammered. "I mean no disrespect, Fabalita. My proposition concerns your passion for the corrida. You must truly love the art of bullfighting to take the risks you did last Sunday."

"I could be the greatest matador in the world if only I had the chance!"

"That's it; I want to give you that chance. How would you like to have the experience of working with a bull in an actual corrida?"

"Dígame, what must I do?"

"Listen. I have a wound in my leg that runs from my crotch almost to my knee. I can barely walk. Yet my manager has me booked for a fight this very Sunday. I am unable to hobble through a paseo, so how can I hope to handle a bull? But, if I break the contract my career is finished."

Esmeralda stirred her coffee. "What has all this to do with me?" she asked. "I'm not your manager."

"No, but you are almost my size; I'm quite short, I admit it. My suit of lights would fit you with no problem. With your hair tied up no one could tell the difference."

"Are you suggesting that I take your place in the arena?"

"Exactamente, Fabalita." Carlos took her hands in his like a suitor. "Will you do it? It goes without saying that my share of the purse will be yours."

Esmeralda's smile eased, costume jewelry once again. "It is only fair," she said, "but even if there was no money I would still say yes."

"Bless you, bless you," Carlos mumbled, kissing the girl's hands. "You have saved my life."

"I will do your reputation no great harm either," Esmeralda said.

Not many blocks from where Carlos and Esmeralda sat with candlelight shining on their greasy faces, Lucky Sam Wo and Don Pepe joined forces over several bottles of Rana de Arbol beer at the empresario's favorite nameless bar. Lucky Sam was buying. He clapped his old friend on the back. "Cheer up, Pepe," he said. "McHaggis knows his job. I trust his information. If the cops haven't got the bull we have nothing to fear. As long as the animal is here in the city and I keep the batteries charged in the radio transmitter there will be no trouble; el toro will remain gentle as a milk cow. And if the woman who bought him has taken him away to the country, out of transmission range, why, he will act as bulls act everywhere and what could be more normal than that? No one will suspect a thing. Believe me, amigo, we're in the clear."

"If you say so, Sammy, I won't argue with you." Don Pepe belched and rubbed his stomach. Beer didn't agree with him. "But still, I'll keep the boys on the lookout. If something turns up, I want to be the first to hear about it."

"Always keep control of the situation, Pepe, that way you make no mistakes."

"I'm in your debt, Sam."

"Yes, in point of fact you are," the Chinaman said. "I did you a big favor, building all that gear and planting the stimuceiver in the bull's brain. There was a certain amount of risk involved, too, as well as expenses. If things didn't work out, it wasn't my fault. But what are friends for, eh, Pepe? And if I helped you maybe you can help me now."

"Anything, Sam, just name it."

Lucky Sam inhaled a pinch of Otterburn snuff. "I made a deal today to run my mechanical bull in the Plaza de Toros. There's no money involved, but I couldn't buy the publicity at any price. All I need now is the right torero."

"Ah, that will be muy difícil. You know how it is with matadors—too much pride. They will turn up their noses at your machine and call it a tin can, a windup toy."

"That is why I come to you, Pepe. What about your boy Chicote?"

"You want Carlos? After seeing him in the ring?"

"I know he's no good," Sam Wo said. "That's not important. I can program the bull to make him look good. What I care about is getting my invention before the public. When people see the robot in action and are unable to tell it from the real thing they will accept it, just as they now accept padded horses. And when the ring managers discover that they can buy one of my machines and use it over and over, Sunday after Sunday, for years on end, it won't take them long to figure out how much money they will save. But I need your bullfight expertise and, to be honest, your connections. I'll make you my partner, Pepe; we can retire to the Canaries and lie on the beach for the rest of our days."

The two old criminals touched glasses and drank, smiling through the foam into beer as mellow and golden as the Tenerife sunset.

domingo próximo

ON SUNDAY MORNINGS Doña Carlota Madrigal was at her post in the bell tower an hour before dawn. The church-yard of Sueño de Duende crowned a poplar-covered hill-side high above the town, and the rising sun lit first the bell tower, next the treetops and, by degrees, the weathered façade of the ancient church. Sunday was a busy time in the churchyard. The earliest arrivals came for six o'clock Mass and there were always a few who lingered among the tombs. Doña Carlota carefully scruti-nized all the mourners with her ten-power binoculars.

A bit after nine, she spotted the rumpled figure of the empresario Don Pepe trudging up the dusty path toward the churchyard. Doña Carlota smiled. When Pepe came by the house yesterday afternoon to pay his respects, she silently let the pompous old fool bluster his way through twenty minutes of awkward small talk before she asked, "Have you been to see Arturo?" The first thing in the morning, he had promised, and as much as Carlota de-tested the man, she was secretly pleased at seeing him keep his word.

Don Pepe stood with his head bowed before the ornate monument housing Arturo Madrigal's mortal remains. After a decent interval, Doña Carlota watched him make the sign of the cross and shuffle off down the gravel walk. She knew the empresario had not influenced her son's decision to abandon a career in science for the bullring, but Pepe was responsible for the bookings, and if he hadn't packed the schedule so full that final season perhaps Arturo might have lived to retire and become the herpetologist God intended him to be.

The sound of voices among the poplars interrupted her speculation: "Is he gone? Can you see?" Doña Carlota raised the field glasses to her yellow eyes with the speed of a striking viper.

"Shhh! I hear his footsteps still."

"Can you see him?"

"No, he's gone out through the gate."

"That was close," a young man said, emerging from the shrubbery. "Who would have expected it at this hour?" Doña Carlota studied his face through the binoculars: a weakling, she decided, a man lacking in pundonor.

The girl who followed him had the haughty look of a gypsy. "Who is he?" she asked.

"Don Pepe, my manager. I don't want him to see the two of us together before the corrida."

The corners of Doña Carlota's mouth tightened with scorn. So this was Pepe's new sword; what a pale shadow compared with her Arturo. On the morning of the corrida, when he should be on his knees in the chapel, here he is, hiding in the bushes with his painted gypsy puta. No wonder Pepe didn't bring him to meet her yesterday afternoon.

"It's over here," the girl called. "The one with the angels."

Doña Carlota watched them approach her son's tomb. The binoculars followed every move.

"Don Pepe was the manager of Arturo Madrigal," the novillero said. "Right until the end."

"Is this true?" The gypsy girl's sullen expression brightened.

"He recognized the same seed of greatness in me, but I have had mal suerte with injuries since my first season."

"I would call your luck fantástico," the girl said, "at being even remotely connected to such nobility. Arturo Madrigal was an artist of the first rank. There was the soul of a poet in his capework."

Carlota Madrigal was sickened to hear these words of praise for her son come from this harlot's mouth. A thing of the gutter; vermin not fit to touch the bottom of Arturo's shoe. What right had she to even breathe his name?

"Look how handsome he was." The girl knelt by the side of the tomb and reached out her hand to touch the statue's marble cheek. "See his noble face. Here was a man without equal."

Doña Carlota ground her teeth in silent fury. She watched through the field glasses as the gypsy whore bent over Arturo's effigy and rubbed her filthy lips against his image. The little puta would die for that! Before the day was out, slowly and without mercy; Doña Carlota vowed to purify her son's defiled memory with the blood of this worthless slut. It was the very least a mother could do.

Mercy Malone ate Sunday breakfast with her bull. Before leaving the house, she filled a thermos with hot tea, and on her way across the city, she bought a half-dozen deep-fried churros from a sidewalk vendor who forked them from his pot of boiling oil and tied them together on a length of flat green reed. El Camión's stall was a pleasant place for a picnic, with lots of clean, dry straw to sit on and the sweet smell of new-mown hay in the air.

Mercy hardly ever saw Paco anymore. She had moved into a guest bedroom at the Machismo town house three nights after he stood her up on a dinner date. There was a picture in the society section of the next morning's newspaper showing him at some posh midtown disco, doing the boogaloo with a recently divorced condesa. Mr. Machismo could shove it for all Mercy cared. If the management of the Francisco Cortina Riding Academy weren't so bloody stuffy, she would ask about sleeping there in the stall with el Camión.

Mercy sat, dunking crisp bits of churro into a cup of tea, and stared at the hulking animal, admiring his sleek strength and the scimitar spread of his fearsome horns. After breakfast she would curry and brush him and rub his hoofs with oil. The top of el Camión's head needed extra grooming, especially the area between the horns, which had a peculiar crooked look, like a woman with her wig askew.

Mercy stood up for a closer examination, dusting greasy churro crumbs from the lap of her tartan maxiskirt. El Camión waited placidly and she stroked the big bull's neck and whispered low murmuring sounds into his ear. Something was definitely wrong with the top of his head. Mercy ran her hand between el Camión's horns and lifted half his scalp as easily as a grounds keeper replaces a worn section of Astroturf.

"Jesus deliver us," the girl gasped, recoiling with horror. But she returned for a closer look, fully expecting a surgeon's-eye view of blood and bone and finding instead only a second layer of bullhide. The scalp she held was a dummy, crudely sewn into place on the bull's head. Underneath, Mercy made another discovery: curling from el Camión's cranium, like sofa springs burst through the upholstery, were a pair of interconnected copper wires.

El Camión trembled with pleasure as the delicate two-legged who smelled of spring flowers rubbed his shoulders and neck. This slight creature had hair the color of sunshine; the color of summer straw; the color of the rolling hills on the ranch where he was born. Lost in his electronic nirvana, the fighting bull perceived the girl as the embodiment of all his most treasured memories. Her smell and color, the bright cornflower blue of her eyes, brought back the happy magic of calfhood. Her caresses recalled the tender touch of his mother's muzzle. The melodic sounds she made were sweeter than birdsong or the purl of spring water over stones. The big animal felt a rush of warmth and joy whenever she entered his stall. El Camión was in love.

When Marty Farb entered the hotel suite of Toro Productions he found Abe Wasserman hidden behind his newspaper, a curl of cigar smoke the only sign that someone was home. "Hey, Marty," Abe called without looking up, "remember Freddie Zink?"

"Sure, Fat Freddie from Canarsie. What about him?"

"He's got a TV pilot that he's promoting now, a daytime quiz giveaway. Just get a load of this: the name of the show is 'You Bet Your Sweet Ass,' and here's the gimmick: the contestants come to the studio with all their valuables, cash, jewels, stock certificates, the deeds to their homes, safe-deposit-box keys, what have you; and they make bets with the m.c. to win prizes, like say, a man might bet his wife's wedding ring for a crack at a brand-new station wagon."

"That sounds like Fat Freddie, all right," Marty Farb said. "When he was making book in Queens back in the old days, he'd take anything you had, including the fillings outta your teeth, to settle a bet."

"Yeah, but this is the best part." Abe scanned the next paragraph in *Variety*. "Listen to this: if a contestant bets his whole bankroll and loses, he still has a chance at the grand prize. On stage, they've got this giant meat cutter, you know, like one of the pastrami slicers at the deli? Only this slicer's got a blade six feet in diameter, sharp as a razor. It can cut paper-thin. The contestant sticks his *tuchas* through the slot and bets by the slice. Each time he misses a question they take off another couple of millimeters. Some babe in a bikini runs the machine. She trims this poor bastard's tushy just like she was building a Reuben sandwich."

"Freddie Zink always wanted his pound of flesh," Marty said, reaching for a cigar. "If there ain't any more hot items, maybe you wanna hear some real news?"

"You got something on the Chink?" Abe folded the copy of *Variety* and tucked it into a desk drawer.

"Naturally. I had Harry do some digging over at Interpol and Professor Chop Suey's got a record as long as your grandfather's underdrawers: thirty-four arrests and no convictions."

Abe whistled in appreciation. "Smart operator," he said. "What sort of charges they got him on?"

"You name it: extortion, conspiracy, counterfeiting; plus he's been an accessory in just about every big heist on the Continent for the past twenty-five years. This is no ordinary one-from-column-A Chinaman; he'll mastermind any caper you come up with for a percentage, plus supply whatever special hardware the job requires. There are a lot of big-time cops who'd give anything for a make on Lucky Sam Wo."

"You know what I'm thinking?" Abe Wasserman asked, contemplating his manicured fingernails. "I'm thinking the Chink is made to order. It was our lucky day when that little fortune cookie walked into the office. The name of the game is 'You Bet Your Sweet Ass,' only this time, the meat in the slot is yellow."

Elsewhere, the empresario Don Pepe was having his problems. What other than bad luck could he expect from a day which began with a visit to a graveyard? He should have known the consequences of hanging around Arturo's tomb on the morning of a corrida. Every time he saw those carved marble angels it brought to mind the repossessed Chrysler. (Surely it was a sacrilege to mourn for a lost limousine while pretending to pray for the soul of a departed friend.) It came as no surprise to Don Pepe that all of his troubles this morning should be automotive.

He paced the oil-stained concrete floor of Sueño de Duende's only garage. Sunday was the mechanics' day off and the place was empty and silent, except for the empresario's echoing footsteps. Garages depressed Don Pepe. The smell of gasoline and rubber filled him with despair.

When the garage owner finished his phone conversation and stepped from his glass-walled office, the empresario hurried over, rubbing his hands imploringly. "What about that big Mercedes up on the rack?" he begged. "I'll pay double."

"Out of the question, Pepe, that's the mayor's car. It's here for a tune-up and a lube job."

"I only need it for an hour or so," the empresario wheedled. "Who would be the wiser?"

"No, Pepe, not even for old times' sake," the garage owner said. "All the money on earth wouldn't tempt me to insult the alcalde by renting his car out to a bullfighter."

"All right, I understand; but you and I have done business so often in the past—tell me again, what happened to the old Alfa I rented for Arturo Madrigal's first fights?"

"A total wreck. The train from Sevilla struck it at the crossroads three years ago. There wasn't enough left over for spare parts."

Don Pepe wrung his hands like a man in pain. "I'll settle for anything, even that yellow Fiat taxicab with the dented fender parked out back."

The garage owner placed his hand consolingly on the empresario's shoulder. "Believe me, Pepe, I would like to help you," he said. "I would give you the taxi for nothing if it were running, but my boys ripped out the transmission only yesterday. I'm afraid the only surviceable vehicle at my disposal is the one we spoke of earlier."

Don Pepe sighed and shook his head. "You know how matadors are, so superstitious. Riding to the arena in such a car as that would surely throw Chicote off his form."

"But it is black and has dignity. It is not a frivolous vehicle, Pepe."

"Claro que sí, it is truly a handsome machine; but it has, shall we say, unpleasant associations."

The garage owner shrugged. "What more can I do, my friend? All my cars are either under contract or in the shop for repair. There's simply nothing else available."

"Then I have no choice," Don Pepe said. "I can't have my boy walk to the arena, how would that look? I'll take it, but at the discount we agreed upon before."

"Naturally," the garage owner said as the two men approached the long black '48 Cadillac hearse parked in the corner. Discreet gray curtains hung in the windows and small silver vases filled with plastic flowers brightened the somber interior. "Look at it this way, Pepe, if all I've read of your boy Chicote is true, you've picked the appropriate vehicle. The novillero can ride up front on the way to the corrida, and in back after our big bulls have finished with him."

"Pull the straps tighter, please." Esmeralda Fabada hung onto a bedpost as Carlos Carretera tugged at the fabric binding her chest.

"Doesn't it hurt you, Fabalita?"

"No. It's much better than having those things flopping around under my shirt." With her breasts strapped flat and her long hair pinned and tied back into a matador's coleta, Esmeralda looked decidedly boyish, although years younger than Carlos, whose features betrayed the rigors of his bohemian existence. "I will have to use some makeup after all," she said, studying her face in the hotel-room mirror, "so I can have sunken cheeks and dark circles under my eyes just like you, Carlos."

A few dabs of eye shadow did the trick. The resemblance, if not perfect, was reasonably exact. The girl and the novillero were almost the same height and weight; both had black hair and brown eyes; even the mole on Carlos's upper lip was duplicated with eyebrow pencil above Esmeralda's more sensuous mouth. "My own mother would be fooled," Carlos said hopefully.

The suit of lights was laid on the bed like the glittering silhouette of a man asleep. Esmeralda dressed slowly, savoring each button of the white lace-front shirt and taking time to get the knot exactly right in the slim silk necktie. She felt Carlos watching her as she sat on the bed and pulled the elastic pink stockings above her knees. The pants were next, knee-length and tassled. Esmeralda adjusted the suspenders and regarded herself in the mirror. A young matador stared back from the depths of the age-flecked glass. "Today I am a stand-in for el Chicote," she thought, reaching for the short embroidered jacket, "but someday soon, I will appear in a traje de luces of my own with my hair down and free: la Fabalita, Queen of the Corrida."

"My own mother—" Carlos repeated.

"Never mind her," Esmeralda snapped. "What about your manager, will he be able to tell?"

"Never. His eyesight is failing but he's too vain to wear spectacles except when reading. If you don't look him straight in the face, he'll never know the difference."

"Bueno. I will leave you now."

"Wait, Fabalita." Carlos stood in front of the door and held up his hand like a traffic policeman. "There's another problem. What about the maid?"

"What about her?"

"She'll see me when she comes in to clean the room," Carlos said. "Everyone in the hotel knows that I am el Chicote. I'm supposed to be at the bullring. The maid will put one and two together and we will be exposed."

"That is a problem," Esmeralda said. "Why don't you hide under the bed?"

Carlos was indignant. "A Carretera does not hide under beds," he sniffed. "Besides, if she's efficient, she'll find me down there when she sweeps the floor."

"What about the closet?"

"Out of the question!"

"Wait a minute," Esmeralda said. "The closet—of course." She hurried to the far corner of the room and threw open the closet door. Hanging on hooks inside were her clothes; her red skirt and white rayon blouse, the fringed maroon shawl her grandmother had given her. "If I'm supposed to be you," she said, "why shouldn't you become me? Here are my clothes, I'm sure they'll fit."

"Me, dress as a woman?"

"Would you prefer hiding under the bed?"

"What about your long hair? Surely it will seem strange that mine is so short."

"You can wear my shawl over your head. Sit facing the window with your back to the door."

"Well, I suppose there's no other choice." Carlos gathered Esmeralda's clothes in his arms and disappeared behind a sun-faded velvet screen. In a few moments he stepped back into view and lifted the hem of the pleated red skirt above his hairy shins in a mock curtsey. "How do I look?" he lisped.

"Well, no sailor would give more than half a pack of cigarettes for you, but you'll fool the maid," Esmeralda said, starting out the door.

"Fabalita, will you do me one more favor?"

"What is it this time?"

"My trousers and jacket, will you leave them with the management to be cleaned? I always do this while I'm at the bullring; aside from my traje de luces, it's the only suit I own."

"*Kreegaaaa!*" Lord Greystoke screamed, hurtling through the jungle on the end of a vine. Cheeta, the faithful chimp, was one vine behind, chattering inanely about bananas. Jane and Boy stood holding coconuts on the bamboo porch of the treehouse. . . .

Sitting in a side aisle of the darkened theater, Paco Machismo munched popcorn and watched a former

Olympic swimmer swing from tree to tree. Paco had never learned to swim; neither could he read, so the subtitles went ignored; but el número uno was deft with languages and knew a good deal more English than the monosyllabic ape man.

At the point in the film where the evil white hunters start a grass fire to stampede grazing herds of eland, elephant and wildebeest toward their ivory-poaching Arab cohorts, Paco sat upright in his seat and studied the screen intently. This was the scene he was waiting for. The black-and-white footage of running animals was real, and the contrast between the stark African landscape and the rubber-plant jungle of the Hollywood set produced a scattered laughter throughout the audience. Paco wasn't laughing. His face was as serious as that of a medical student observing a hysterectomy.

A process shot of Tarzan scanning the burning horizon; cut to: stampeding zebras beneath a flaming thorn tree; cut to: elephants trumpeting; and now—it was coming again at last, and Paco held his breath—cut to: three browsing rhinoceroses. The first caught a scent of smoke and lifted his two-pronged head. Slowly, the huge beast began to trot. The others followed at a slow shuffle.

Paco edged forward on his seat, spilling popcorn and licking his dry lips. The rhinoceros broke into a full headlong gallop, charging blindly across the open plain. For such bulky creatures, it was amazing how fast they ran. Paco was sweating in the refrigerated air of the movie theater. This was the third time he had seen the film today.

The harsh, inhospitable landscape of Extremadura breeds a people accustomed to endurance and hardship. Out of the poverty of this arid and unforgiving region was born a race of conquistadors: Cortez, Balboa, the Pizarro brothers, all were extremeños. The faces of the spectators who crowded the small bullring on the outskirts of Sueño de Duende were stamped with the same stern determination. One look at their flinty eyes and firm, unsmiling mouths recalled civilizations put to the torch, a noble race enslaved, Sun Kings at swordpoint. The empresario Don Pepe Bacalao y Piñas watched the somber crowd fill the arena and knew that he could expect no sympathy here for el Chicote's clumsiness.

The novillero had been acting strangely all afternoon. When the empresario picked Carlos up at the hotel he had expected one of those excesses of temperament which for the young man served to mask a total lack of valor. But the matador said not a word at the sight of the hearse. He entered the unlucky vehicle without complaint and rode up front next to the driver, staring sullenly out of the window all the way to the Plaza de Toros.

And in the bullring el Chicote had ignored the empresario from the start. Usually, before a fight, Don Pepe spent every available minute consoling the trembling torero, whispering encouragement into his ear and reassuring him of success, but today el Chicote wanted no part of him, preferring the idle gossip of the monosabios to his own cogent advice.

The corrida at Sueño de Duende was strictly the minor leagues, with only one picador in attendance and the matadors placing their own banderillas. The paseo was a ragtag affair, almost a parody of big-city processions, and Don Pepe watched the motley parade, tempering his melancholy with memories of Arturo Madrigal beginning his career in the same provincial bullring. El Chicote always looked good in the paseo. Marching in parades suited his fraudulent dramatic nature and Don Pepe looked on ruefully as his boy strutted across the arena. "If only they awarded ears and tails for marching in formation," the empresario thought with an unhappy sigh.

As the novillero with senior standing among the three nonentities fighting today, el Chicote drew the first bull, a monstrous spotted creature well over five years of age. From the experienced, menacing way he slowly circled the arena it was obvious that the animal had been fought before in the amateurs. Don Pepe groaned and cradled his head in his arms on top of the barrera. The medical bills would surely absorb every céntimo of the scanty purse.

Don Pepe watched el Chicote stride valorously to the center of the arena and incite the bull with a sharp stamp of his foot. Where were the trembling knees, the ashen face? The boy must be drunk. The first pass, a serene veronica, brought a loud "Olé" from the crowd and the cheering increased in volume as the precise and delicate capework continued. The empresario watched as if in a dream; it was almost like seeing the first performances of Arturo Madrigal once again.

Don Pepe hurried to speak with Carlos at the conclusion of his faena when the boy walked to the barrera to wipe his sweating face and take a drink of water, but el Chicote was back in the arena before he could reach him, skillfully maneuvering the bull into position for the picador. The loyalty of the spectators was insured when the novillero waved the pikeman off after only two thrusts of the lance.

Don Pepe's amazement grew along with the crowd's enthusiasm as el Chicote gracefully placed three pairs of banderillas, each pair from increasingly difficult terrain until the last two went in with the young matador's back against the barrera. El Chicote dedicated the bull to his cheering audience and went to work immediately with the muleta and sword. While the boy's early capework had been elegant fantasy, his performance with the cloth had the calm, unhurried dignity of tragedy. Naturals, pases de pecho, concertinas, cucarachas de gamba: all the most demanding passes in the repertory, joined together seemingly without effort. The spectators howled their "Olés." Don Pepe was certain he was witnessing a miracle.

When the moment came for the kill, a hush fell over the arena. An inept sword stroke would ruin all the beauty which had gone before and the anticipation in the Plaza de Toros was almost palpable. The matador profiled the bull, standing very straight and sighting along the heavy curved blade of his sword. A slight gesture with the muleta provoked the bull's charge and the crowd gasped as the huge animal impaled himself on the extended sword. Chicote leaned on the weapon and it sank to its flannel-wrapped hilt between the brute's muscled shoulders.

The matador jumped back, arms spread in triumph, as the bull swayed and went down, all four legs in the air. The spectators were screaming, hurling hats, flowers and botas into the arena in celebration. Don Pepe felt drunk with joy. Then, before the astonished eyes of the jubilant crowd, the young novillero's shining black hair shifted and fell, tumbling in glossy waves almost to his waist.

The cheering stopped while near a thousand mouths hung in open amazement at this incredible transformation. "It's a woman," someone called from the stands.

"It's la Fabalita!" cried another, who followed the bull-fight news from the capitol. "Sí, sí, Fabalita," the spectators agreed as the cheering resumed, louder than before, and as the first enthusiastic young men jumped into the arena and rushed to lift their heroine triumphantly onto their shoulders, the cry grew near-hysterical: *"Faba-litaaaaaaa . . . !"*

The empresario applauded behind the barrera. He had no rational explanation for this miraculous transmutation, but he accepted it with the aplomb of a fairy-tale milk-maid witnessing the unexpected change of frog into prince. Whatever the explanation, Don Pepe knew his fortune was assured. Before the afternoon was out he would have la Fabalita's signature drying on a contract.

Doña Carlota Madrigal waited in the shade of a cork tree in the plaza, across from the entrance of the Hotel Ambiente. She sat on a wrought-iron bench with a knitting bag open on her lap. Her narrow yellow eyes never blinked. She watched as Don Pepe and his novillero left the hotel and drove off in a rented hearse.

The chimes in the little chapel opposite the plaza tolled away each quarter-hour and still she sat, observing the crowd passing along the street on the way to the bullring. As the time for the corrida approached, the sidewalks grew deserted. Only a few last-minute stragglers hurried past the Hotel Ambiente; and when the distant call of the trumpet carried across the rooftops of Sueño de Duende, there was not a single soul in sight.

Doña Carlota closed her knitting bag and rose sinu-ously to her feet. Without a sound, she glided across the plaza and crossed the empty street. She avoided the lobby of the Hotel Ambiente, sidling around cautiously to the service entrance in the rear. Bales of dirty linen were piled outside the laundry room, but the washerwoman had abandoned her scrubbing to steal off to the bullfight.

Inside, Doña Carlota found a stack of maids' uniforms,

freshly starched and ironed. Within seconds she was buttoned into one of the iron-gray smocks and had knotted a black apron around her waist. A dark-blue kerchief concealed her hair, and over her nose and mouth she wore, as she had seen the other maids do, a broad gauze dust mask. She shoved her knitting bag into a large pocket in the apron and, taking a mop from the broom closet, started for the back stairs.

On the third-floor landing, in a small metal cabinet above the fire extinguisher, Doña Carlota found the passkey. Silently, she hurried down the hallway, her slippered feet sliding across the worn carpet. A phone call to the desk that morning had yielded the correct room number and she paused for a moment outside the door and looked both ways down the deserted corridor before quietly slipping the key into the lock.

The gypsy puta didn't bother to turn her proud head as Doña Carlota entered. The little trollop sat with her back to the door, covered by a shawl like a woman in church.

"Perdóneme, señorita, I will take but a minute to prepare the bed and sweep the floor." Doña Carlota reached into the pocket of her apron and withdrew a slender steel knitting needle. The haughty bitch ignored her. Not fit for decent work herself and yet too proud to exchange a few words with the maid. Doña Carlota clenched her teeth in a cobra's frozen smile and leaned the mop against the wall. "Is the señorita not feeling well?" she hissed. "I felt surely she would accompany her novio to the corrida."

The slut by the window only coughed in reply as Doña Carlota moved stealthily across the room, the needle gripped like an abbreviated rapier in her right hand. She stood for a moment behind the seated girl, completely still, her yellow eyes glittering in cold fury. Then, reaching out quickly, Doña Carlota seized the gypsy wench by the neck with her left hand and drove the stiletto-sharp knitting needle deep into her temple with her right.

The girl made a sound halfway between a yelp and a whimper and slumped to the floor, the steel needle standing straight up out of her head like a radio antenna. Doña Carlota reached down and tugged the maroon shawl away for a closer look. Now it was her turn to yelp.

This wasn't the gypsy girl, it was Don Pepe's novillero! A thin line of blood ran down his cheek and puddled in the socket of his staring eye. Doña Carlota was truly horrified. She was a simple countrywoman and unaccustomed to perversions. Although she had read of such things in the tabloids, this was the first time she had ever seen a transvestite with her own eyes. Señora Madrigal sat down in the chair recently occupied by the corpse on the floor and said five quick Ave Marias to regain her composure.

viernes

"Come in, come in, please." Lucky Sam Wo bowed like the number one son and ushered his American visitors into his studio. "I am honored, gentlemen."

"Quite a place you got here, professor." Abe Wasserman drifted through the room in a blue nimbus of cigar smoke.

"A regular Gyro Gearloose," was Marty Farb's comment.

"Chiro Girluz?" Sam Wo frowned. "I am not familiar with this person, Girluz."

"A famous American inventor," Abe said, "beloved by schoolchildren from coast to coast. Tell the professor what a thrill this is for us, Marty."

"This is a real thrill for us, prof," Marty said. "You live in this place or only work here?"

"My work and my life are one. The happiest mechanic never closes his toolbox."

"You must be very happy then," Abe said. "I never seen so much equipment scattered around one place before."

"A tool for every purpose," Sam Wo said. "I like to keep

many projects going at once. In this way, industry creates the illusion of chaos."

"Where do you hide this mechanical bull of yours, prof?" Marty studied the disarray spread across a workbench with the air of a man looking in the little windows at the Automat.

"It's quite large, you know, and gets in the way, so, when not in use, it resides in storage." Lucky Sam pointed over a dusty stack of cardboard cartons toward the rear of the studio. "But there is more room here in the front. Better for viewing. You wait, I will bring the machine."

"Before you do, professor," Abe said, "I have a couple of papers here I'd like you to sign." He opened a legal-sized leather envelope and stacked a number of documents on the corner of the workbench.

"Papers? What is the nature of these papers?"

"Just some standard release forms, prof. You know, absolving Toro Productions from any responsibility for damage caused by your robot. And a contract, stating that we don't owe you anything; that you got no claims on us. It's all like we talked about back at the office."

Sam Wo pulled on his spectacles and scrutinized the legal forms. "Everything looks in order," he said. "Where do I sign?"

"Here." Abe pointed. "And here on the other side, and here . . . and right here. I guess that does it, professor, or should I say partner?"

Abe and Lucky Sam shook hands as vigorously as politicians at the opening of a shopping center. "Partner!" They smiled in harmony.

"My friends, it will take only a short time to show you the machine," said the Chinese inventor. "Please make yourself comfortable and I will return in, how do you say? a jiffy."

Abe and Marty were all smiles. They waited until Lucky Sam was out of earshot in the back of his studio before Abe whispered, "Got what you need?"

"It's a piece of cake," Marty said. "The lock on the door is a standard Conklin type with a reverse spring action. I could open it with a credit card. No alarm system of any kind that I can see. How are the signatures?"

"Nice and firm; lifting an impression should be simple."

Marty chuckled. "What a perfect setup. There's enough stuff around here for a make without even planting a thing. I counted three different calibre silencers on the workbench: real beauties. And last time I seen one of them magnetic alarm deactivators was when Louis Bepe and Champagne Eddie were in the fur-heist business."

"Shhh!" Abe held a warning finger to his lips. "I hear the Chink coming."

It was the automated bull, moving in a slow bovine shuffle, head down and lowing. Lucky Sam walked behind like a drover. In his hand he carried a compact control unit, the size and shape of a pocket calculator. The robot animal lumbered past the astonished American producers and came to a stop by the door.

"That's incredible, professor," Abe said. "I could swear it was breathing."

"If we were outside in the park you could see it run."

"What's wrong with its head?" Marty investigated a space between the horns where a square section of hide was missing. The shine of machine-tooled steel showed from underneath.

"A final detail as yet unfinished," Sam Wo said. "The taxidermist is coming this afternoon with a piece made to order."

"How many of these bulls you got, professor?" Abe asked. "A whole herd?"

"No, no, this prototype is the only one I've built."

"That's strange," Marty said, "I could swear the toreador's girl friend bought some kind of mechanical toro. Didn't Paco say it had a bunch of wire sticking out of its head?"

Lucky Sam Wo's almond eyes brightened. "Excuse please, would you be more explicit? Whose girl friend has a bull with wires in its head?"

"Paco Machismo, the bullfighter we hired," Abe said. "He's been shacking up with this teen-age singer, some Irish chick. She bought herself a genuine Spanish fighting bull to show the folks back home; only it's got wires in its head just like yours, professor."

"How curious. If you would give me the girl's name, I would like very much to examine this peculiar animal."

"Figure someone's beat you to the punch? The mechanical bull business turns out to be pretty competitive, don't it, Marty?"

"Looks that way," Marty said.

"Gentlemen, I guarantee you that my invention is unique," Sam Wo pushed a button and his bull nuzzled Marty Farb's cheek. "Nevertheless, I'm sure you both will agree that it would be foolhardy not to look into the matter."

"Professor, it never hurts to know what the other guy is up to; that's rule number one in any business."

"Nunca!" Paco Machismo stamped his foot. The crack of his heel against the parquet was as final as a slamming door. "Never, it is an impossibility."

His manager, Alfredo Gazpacho, simply shrugged. "But Paco, what can we do? The contracts are signed."

"I spit on all contracts."

"It's five hundred thousand U.S. dollars, Paco."

"I spit on money of any denomination."

"Paco—"

"And I spit on those who manage money—whose minds are poisoned by its touch."

"Don't count your bridges before they're burned, Paco. And as for your spit, save it for the arena where the crowd enjoys a show of valor." Gazpacho settled with an exasperated sigh onto the padded leather of a Miës van der Rohe Barcelona chair. "How can you be so arrogant?" he asked softly. "What were you before you had any money? A bakery boy who couldn't read or write, who slept on the dirt floor behind the bread ovens. You still haven't learned to read or write, although you spend a fortune for tutors; but I suspect the silk sheets on your bed are more comfortable than sleeping on cardboard."

"I've earned what is mine." Paco folded his arms and glowered out the window.

"I'm not denying that. It's your petty tantrums I'm tired of; your refusal to face the realities of life. What have you got, Paco, that is worth more than money?"

"My honor."

"Ah, his precious honor." Alfredo Gazpacho threw up his arms and gazed soulfully at the ornate ceiling like the disposessed heroine in a melodrama. "And this code of honor which rules your life has a regulation about appearing on the same bill with a woman: you are a regular Knight Templar, Paco."

"Of course it is a dishonor for a matador to fight alongside a woman. Only a fool whose brain has gone to fat with too much money would fail to see that."

Mercy Malone's lilting laughter pealed across the room. She sat on a piano bench in the corner where she'd been working out with the baby grand before the business conference intervened. "Right on, brother," she giggled. "El cerdo chauvenístico."

"There, you see." Paco Machismo pointed with his sword arm. "Listen to that. Should any man share his moment of glory with a creature like that?"

"Shee-it," Mercy jeered.

"It's your decision, Paco," his manager said quietly. "Your honor, I'm certain, will tolerate the things people will say about you."

"Such things as what?"

"Oh, that you're a coward; that Paco Machismo was afraid to face the rinoceronte in the arena."

"My people wouldn't say that, not after I give my word and pledge my honor . . ."

"I wouldn't be so seguro, my young friend," Gazpacho said, getting slowly to his feet. "The public has a shorter attention span than you do. It won't take them very long to start looking for a new hero. They're very fond of la Fabalita already. Songs are sung about her in the cantinas. Perhaps she'll fight the rhinoceros in your place. Think it over, Paco."

"I won't do it!" Esmeralda Fabada stamped her foot. The slap of her bare toes against the tiles was soundless. "I don't care what arrangements have been made, I say no. And again, one thousand times: *No!*"

Her manager, the empresario Don Pepe, considered how pleasant it would be to beat her with his belt. "My dear child," he crooned, "think of what you're saying. It's the chance of a lifetime."

"It is a disgraceful mockery of the art."

"How many matadors with only one small-town novillado to their credit have the opportunity to appear in La

Plaza de Toros Municipal on the same cartel with Paco Machismo?"

"How many matadors are asked to fight an adding machine? If I wanted to be a clown, I would have joined the circus."

"Fabalita, it's not an adding machine; I said it was controlled by computer. It's a marvel, truly. When you see it with your own eyes you won't believe it. The mechanism is every centimeter a bull."

"I don't care if it's every centimeter a camel, I won't do it."

Don Pepe spoke in a whisper. "It doesn't matter what you care, we have a contract, you and I."

"To hell with your contract," Fabalita screamed. "Where is it? I'll tear it up. You can't make me do it if I say no."

"That's true, I can't force you." Don Pepe never raised his voice. "But the contract is a legal document, duly signed and recorded, and it gives me full control of your career for the next twenty-five years. You can never work for anybody else. Now you have a glorious future, Fabalita, if you do as I say. However, if you refuse to cooperate, it's finished; you go back on the streets. Which will it be, Fabalita, the bullring or the brothel? The choice is up to you."

"How good of you to come, señorita." Lucky Sam Wo tipped his dove-gray homburg, half rising as he motioned the lithe blond pop star to have a seat beside him under the parasol. "Will you take some coffee?"

Mercy Malone said, "You know, I don't usually accept invitations from strange men, but when you said on the phone that you wanted to talk about el Camión, well, I've got to admit I was interested. How did you find out about my bull in the first place?"

"That is a long and extremely uninteresting story," Lucky Sam said, filling her cup with coffee. "What is more to the point is the history of the animal itself. I suspect you must be curious about the wires in his head?"

"Very."

"The explanation is simple. El Camión was a guinea pig in a medical experiment to control psychomotor epilepsy. A radio transmitter has been surgically implanted in the bull's brain. This device greatly affects his behavior. He was being shipped to Madrid for further study at our facilities here when the railroad mixed up the invoices and put him in with a load bound for the bullring by mistake."

"So that explains why he acts so peaceful."

"Exactly. You can turn him on or off—by that I mean alter his behavior from aggressive to passive—by merely pushing a button. Someday governments will require everybody to wear a device like this in his brain. No more aggression or violence; a central computer will keep everything peaceful."

"Sounds awful," Mercy said.

"I can imagine worse possible futures."

"Don't lay your bad trips on me. You'll probably be getting royalties when everybody else is plugged into one of those little gadgets."

"The patents are the property of the Medical Institute," Sam Wo said testily. "My profit comes from benefiting mankind."

"I suppose you called me because you want your bull back," Mercy sulked.

"Not exactly. It would be extremely embarrassing to the Institute if word of this were to get out. Four people were killed, you must remember. In fact, there's a very good chance that Government funds for the project would be cut off. And you, of course, would lose the bull.

"However, I'm certain there's a reasonable solution. You want to keep the bull; we want you to keep our secret. A simple handshake will assure both."

"You got a deal, doc," Mercy said, clasping his pale yellow fingers.

"Of course, now that the animal is yours, I'm sure you'll be interested in the controls." Lucky Sam pulled a small black suitcase from under the circular table and opened it on his lap. "It's quite uncomplicated," he said. "This switch is the main control. When the unit is on, the bull will remain passive. When the current is switched off, he reverts to his instinctive behavior. This knob on the left allows the operator to control the transition gradually: at one end of the scale, the bull is a zombie; at the other, a savage killer. You can tune him in anywhere in between."

"That's fab," Mercy said. "Absolutely super. How much for a set of controls?"

Lucky Sam Wo leaned forward like a dining-car conspirator on the Orient Express. "You must remember that my salary at the Institute is a pittance, barely enough to live on. Under those circumstances, I am willing to offer this control unit to you for a mere three hundred pounds sterling."

Mercy reached for her traveler's checks. "Sold," she said.

"You'll never regret it, señorita." Sam Wo smiled.

The tack room of the Francisco Cortina Riding Academy was empty. But anyone hiding among the polished saddles and bridles when Mercy Malone slipped in the side door would have assumed from her trim charcoal-

gray pants suit and black attaché case that a young busi-
nesswoman had come to call. Mercy's manner was decidedly businesslike. She marched down the aisle between
the empty stalls like a corporate vice-president on her way
to a sales conference. There was no nonsense about her
determined stride.

The comatose fighting bull hulked within the strict
confines of his stall, a mother lode of unmined porter-
houses, tenderloins and T-bones. Mercy leaned against
the heavy wooden gate and gazed at the brutish animal
with unfeigned affection. "You lovable hunk of meat," she
whispered, reaching over to pat the glossy rump. "I'm
going to turn you on today, babe."

Mercy set the attaché case on top of the gate and
unsnapped the fasteners. With the lid up, the inside of the
case looked like the dashboard of Paco's Maserati; a row
of dials nested in pebble-grained leather. Mercy's hand
paused on the calibrated knob. She knew she should wake
the remote-controlled bull by degrees, bringing him to no
more than half-power on a trial run. Yet, her impulse was
always to floor it and she reached out a manicured finger
and flipped the toggle switch to Off.

El Camión awoke with a grunt. Swift as pain, the
dream ended: a dream as innocent as calfhood, as soft and
protective as the enclosing contours of the womb, as
sweet as the first taste of springtime clover. Instead of
bliss, the fighting bull felt rage. His peace and well-being
were cauterized by instant, searing hatred. The narrow
stall, an infinite space only moments before, seemed con-
stricting and oppressive. El Camión wanted out.

Bellowing like a diesel express, the enraged bull drove
his horns into the hay manger and kicked with his hind

legs. The wooden gate burst from its hinges, exploding into kindling under the onslaught of his terrible hoofs. Bucking and plunging, el Camión backed from the stall. He roared in triumph, slinging slobber in all directions as he slashed the air with his horns.

Beneath his feet a two-legged lay pinned by the shattered boards. El Camión reared back, ready for the kill, when a faint smell of flowers made him pause. The fighting bull lowered his muzzle and sniffed the straw-colored hair. A fleeting tenderness calmed his black heart. Faint memories of love were a balm for his anger. He reached out his long, rough tongue and licked the girl's pale cheek. Her skin tasted like violets.

At that moment, two exercise boys leading an Arabian mare entered the stable. El Camión looked up and snorted at this unexpected intrusion. One of the boys screamed and pointed. The mare reared in panic, white showing around her fear-widened eyes. El Camión lowered his horns and charged headlong down the straw-littered aisle, intent upon destruction.

Don Pepe detested funerals. The sight of a coffin chilled his heart. The Latin murmurings of the priest were an immersion in sorrow. Standing in the last row of mourners with his eyes on the ground between his feet, the empresario listened to the somber fall of the clods, pebbles rattling along the polished mahogany lid. The name carved as cleanly as the title of a book across the small white stone read CARLOS CARRETERA. No mention of el Chicote here. The boy in the box wore a dark-blue suit and held a rosary in his folded hands.

The parents, sitting stern and dry-eyed on folding chairs at the gravesite, had not wanted the traje de luces, ordering it burned. Instead, Don Pepe took it to a tailor for alteration to Fabalita's measurements: a resurrection of sorts.

When the obsequies were done and the little crowd divided into groups of two and three in the slow walk to the gate, the empresario caught sight of the father and waved at him with his walking stick. "My sympathies, señor," he said as the angular man approached.

"Gracias. But it was no surprise." The father wiped his thin, bloodless lips with a handkerchief. "No doubt you were anticipating this occasion for several years, as were my wife and myself. He was always clumsy, even as a child; tripping over his shoelaces all day long."

"Sad but true, alas," Don Pepe sighed. "He knew the horns of a bull as well as any man."

"A horn has too much dignity; a knitting needle was more appropriate for Carlos."

"You're unforgiving, Señor Carretera. He was a fine lad. Has the investigation uncovered anything?"

"Bah! The investigation was a mere formality. The Guardia ruled it a crime of passion and went through the motions of questioning three known deviants in the area—all released for lack of evidence. The case remains open, but those who were working on it have been reassigned. I can understand their reluctance; exterminating an abnormality like Carlos is almost a public service."

"It should ease your heart to learn that Carlos was innocent of any unnatural behavior," the empresario said. "La Fabalita went to the corrida in your son's place. They merely exchanged clothing for the afternoon."

"Of course I know that, you old fool, but why inflate the disgrace? There's more honor in dying as a maricón than as a coward."

. . .

Crawling on her elbows, Mercy Malone struggled to get free of the wreckage. Clouds of sunlit hay dust enclosed the shadow-play mayhem ahead. Somewhere a horse was screaming. The attaché case lay upended in a manure pile several feet away and Mercy crawled toward it, praying that the controls were not damaged. She hauled herself up the mountainside of turds like an organic gardener in compost heaven. The slim black case was within her grasp and she lunged for it, smearing her pretty Top Twenty face as she frantically wiped the controls clean and flipped the switch to On. "Work, you bloody box. Oh, please work."

The sounds of pandemonium changed. Although the frenzied hoof-clatter of the frightened horse and the shrieking of the frightened men continued to punctuate the swirling dust, the thunder was definitely gone from the storm. Mercy closed the lid of the attaché case and picked herself out of the fertilizer. Taking care not to breathe too deeply, she hurried down the aisle to inspect the damage.

She found one stable boy clinging to a post. The other hung to the reins of the rearing horse. Somehow, the mare had backed into a side stall and escaped with nothing more than a horn slash on her hindquarters. El Camión stood, struck by lightening, but as far as Mercy could tell, otherwise unhurt. "It's all right, boys," she said to the terrified stable hands, "I've got everything under control. It's all a matter of discipline."

The slim Irish girl led a docile fighting bull back to his stall, and two former jockeys, one still treed to a post like a terrified alley cat, found it hard to come up with the words expressing their true feelings.

· · ·

Doña Carlota Madrigal enjoyed having afternoon coffee in the dry heat of her cactus garden. Seneca, the scrimshawed Galápagos tortoise, served as a slumbering footstool and the señora relaxed with her newspaper, the rustle of turning pages starting numbers of rattlesnakes whirring in the glass cases behind her. A pair of gila monsters scurried along a terrarium ledge, their claws leaving faint bird-marks in the sand.

Since Sunday, Doña Carlota had followed the newspaper carefully, reading it front page to back for word of the murder investigation. After three days, the story no longer rated space even in the second section. Instead, she found a half-page ad for the coming corrida with the rhinoceros. Below all the boldface and the bring-em-back-alive photo, a small blurb caught her raptor's eye. It said:

✿ ✿ ✿ ✿ ✿

In Addition! The New Sensation! LA FABALITA *Testing her skill against the marvel of the* SPACE AGE. . . . . . *the Magnífico! Mecánico!* MOTOTORO!!!!!!

✿ ✿ ✿ ✿ ✿ ✿ ✿

Doña Carlota held her breath as she read, and when she finished, the hiss of her exhale caused the tortoise to open his ancient eye. "So, Fabalita," she whispered, "we meet again."

When Señora Madrigal heard the marketplace gossip detailing the girl's triumph on Sunday, she knew it would be no problem finding her; loose talk travels like a river in flood. Still, it was a surprise to read in the newspaper what she expected to learn while haggling over a cabbage or a kilo of onions.

Doña Carlota rose to her feet, casting the newspaper aside. "I must pack for a trip to Madrid," she told the caseful of snakes. "No, I can't take you, my handsome friends, you're much too noisy. Buzz, buzz, buzz, all day long."

In among the orchids, the señora found something more silent. She carried a specially constructed wicker travel case through the sultry greenhouse to a small wire-mesh cage near the crocodile pit. Lifting the lid, Doña Carlota fished inside with a short, noosed stick and snared a writhing trophy: the lethal Gaboon viper. The harlequin-colored serpent coiled about the stick and probed the air with his tongue. "Hello, my pretty one," she said. "I've found you a bride at last. You must go in this box for a while, precious, but your wedding night will come soon enough. Save your kisses until then."

otro domingo

A MAP OF THE PARADE ROUTE had been published in all three metropolitan dailies, and crowds began gathering along the designated streets as early as six that morning. By noon, there wasn't a free square meter of curbstone to be found all the way from the railroad terminal to the bullring. Candy vendors and panhandlers long accustomed to empty pockets were staggering under the weight of their spare change.

Anything resembling a rhinoceros was an instant success. Rhinoceroses bobbed on balloons and fluttered on a thousand hand-held pennants. Sticky-faced children sucked rhino-shaped lollipops and nibbled bite-size rhinoceros cookies. Adults leafed through African wildlife comic books, pinned plastic rhinoceroses to their hats and tooted mournfully on brand-new rhinoceros whistles. Many could be seen wearing rhinoceros masks, prodding one another with papier-mâché horns.

Abe Wasserman and Marty Farb had several differences of opinion concerning the parade. Marty felt that it should have the spirit of an old-time circus procession:

steam calliopes and brass bands, gilt chariots, lots of P.T. Barnum hoopla. Abe insisted the dagos would never go for it: not enough dignity. He showed Marty postcards of the Semana Santa solemnities in Sevilla to prove his point: hundreds of hooded penitentes, like a Ku Klux Konga line.

Abe got the job and handled all the production details. A phalanx of flag-bearers led the grand event. The banners of every province were on display. This was followed by a smart-stepping drum and bugle corps, keeping things moving, the cadence precise and military. Troops of soldiers in close formation, automatic rifles slung from their shoulders, marched at either end of the horse-drawn wagon. The ornate wheeled cage was rented from a traveling circus, but Abe had the workmen swathe the gilded plaster putti in black satin to insure a proper dignity.

The rhinoceros was borne majestically along, pig-eyed and somber, like an ICBM in the May Day parade. The big African animal never flinched or blinked as crowds of excited madrileños whistled and hurled roasted peanuts. Those who had not been able to buy tickets at the arena paid as much as five times face value when several dozen scalpers milked the anxious crowd. Abe and Marty had made sure to withhold five thousand tickets from the original sale and had hired the scalpers on commission. This was one business decision they agreed upon completely.

In a distant part of the city, Lucky Sam Wo, not invited by Toro Productions to take part in their parade, staged his own private cavalcade, attracting a few curious bystanders and a mob of noisy children trooping along behind. With his legs folded in the lotus position, Lucky Sam rode on the back of his mechanical bull like a mail-order Brahma. A blue silk drape hung down over the robot's flanks, MOTOTORO embroidered in foot-high gold letters on either side. A hidden tape recorder blared bullfight music. Lucky Sam held his invention to a brisk trot, scattering leaflets every half-block or so on his way to the arena.

El Camión was going on a trip. The vet stopped by to see him early in the morning for a round of inoculations. A team of carpenters took his measurements and could be heard hammering in the courtyard of the Francisco Cortina Riding Academy. A specially designed safety harness was fitted and sewn by the saddlemaker, a padded collar and yoke such as no fighting bull ever wore before.

Insulated from indignity by a wall of electrodes, el Camión took true bovine pleasure in these and other two-legged attentions. His big wet eyes shone with doglike affection. After a lifetime of acting tough, el Camión wanted to make friends.

Mercy's morning was spent setting up appointments. First thing after breakfast, she telephoned Paco from the extension in the downstairs hall and told him she was leaving. He mumbled, "Bon voyage," his voice congested with sleep, and that was that. In the next hour, drawing on skills not apparent during the three months she spent at a Liverpool secretarial school before making it big, Mercy called the vet, carpenters to build the crate, a travel agency, the saddlemaker, several shipping firms, two hairdressers and her connection. She arranged a schedule and issued instructions, dovetailing appointments with the logbook precision of an admiral, a call girl or an orthodontist.

Cradling the phone for the final time, Mercy sent the maid upstairs to pack her things and turned to the Ministry of Agriculture forms she had picked up yesterday afternoon at the British consulate: Livestock Importation

Permit Application. She placed those pages to be signed by the veterinarian in a separate folder, uncapping her felt-tipped pen to contemplate the complexities of the remaining form.

Name, age and occupation were easy to fill in; ditto address, place of birth and passport number. More difficult were queries concerning the animal's weight, age, bloodlines; and she left those spaces blank. "Ask vet," she penned in the margin. She puzzled longest over the part which began: Purpose of Importation. Mercy chewed her thumbnail, pained by thought, and when the answer came it was from out of nowhere, like finding the word in an acrostic, and she printed the letters all in capitals as requested: Purpose of Importation . . . BREEDING. Mercy was not without a sense of humor.

Paco Machismo slept late. It was past midday when he crawled from the circular bed and rang for his man-servant. Andrés appeared promptly with an iced pitcher of fresh Valencia orange juice. Paco never ate on the day of a fight. An empty gut kept him alert and was a wise precaution in a profession where surgery was always imminent.

The marble bathroom was as ornate as a Roman mausoleum; the tub, a full-length sarcophagus carved from a single block of stone. While Paco bathed and shaved, his man Andrés opened the velour drapes and laid out a blue suit of lights on the bed. Paco owned two dozen of these jeweled costumes. They hung sparkling in the walk-in closet like the wardrobe of a Grand Ole Opry star.

From a vast mahogany haberdasher's bureau beside the shoe rack, Andrés brought a lace-front shirt, a pair of silk hose, a pin-on coleta, a slender black necktie and six embroidered handkerchiefs which Paco would roll up into a ball and stuff into the crotch of his tight-fitting pants. When it came to a public display of cojones, Paco Machismo refused to take the back seat for any bull.

In a small hotel room in another part of town, la Fabalita dressed herself without the help of servants. The traje de luces was a hand-me-down from el Chicote; she had worn it the week before and the fit was perfect, but Don Pepe had taken it to a tailor and had it recut in a more feminine fashion. The vest and jacket were tailored to emphasize her upthrust breasts; knee britches clung tight as sequined skin.

La Fabalita stared unhappily into the wardrobe mirror. Staring back was a member of the chorus line in a sleazy nightclub bullfight revue. "What a wretched beginning for a career as an artist," the girl thought. "A tick-tock bull and a showgirl outfit; they want Marilyn Monroe, not a matador de toros."

Doña Carlota Madrigal climbed the stairs to her third-floor pension, a gift box of long-stemmed roses cradled in her arms. The family had just finished clearing away the luncheon dishes when she entered. Several boarders sat drinking coffee at the long crumb-covered table. The eldest daughter, busy sweeping the floor, nodded gravely as she passed.

Inside her room, the señora turned the key in the lock and carried her flowers over to the bed. There was a gift envelope attached to the ribbon on the lid of the box and Doña Carlota scrawled a quick inscription: "For la Fabalita, from her greatest admirer."

The roses, redder than blood, lay in the long white box, folded in a cone of green tissue paper. The room filled with their delirious sweetness. Doña Carlota picked a single blossom and breathed its fragrance. A thoughtful florist had trimmed the roses of thorns. "You've lost your sting, beauty," the señora crooned, returning the flower to the box. "Much too frail and lovely to go unprotected. My friend's bite is sharper than yours ever was. Be patient and I will bring him."

Señora Madrigal took the woven wicker traveling case from inside the armoire and brought it to the bedside table. She opened the lid and reached inside with the snare-stick, slipping the noose over the head of the coiled and dormant viper. The snake came writhing out of its slumber.

"Awake, my darling," Doña Carlota said. "Your bridal bouquet is waiting." As she turned with the snare-stick held in both hands, the heel of her slipper caught in the weave of the throw rug. Instantly off-balance, the señora lurched forward, tripping over her own feet, and fell face down across the bed.

It felt like molten metal searing her flesh. Señora Madrigal sat up without an outcry and saw the squirming snake, still securely noosed, beside her on the bed. Without hesitation, she unbuttoned her bodice and pulled down her shirtwaist and chemise. Beneath her left breast she saw the fangs' twin incision, the surrounding skin already pink and swelling.

Her decision was made without debate. There were no alternatives. A doctor was out of the question, even if medical attention could save her now, which she doubted. She had perhaps two hours of life remaining; time enough to reach the bullring. The corrida began in an hour; if she conserved her strength she would make it.

Rising slowly to her feet, she picked up the hog-nosed Gaboon viper and dropped it wriggling among the roses. She closed the lid and tied a bow in the satin ribbon, humming a mournful Castilian melody as she felt the poison spread like a circle of devouring ants across her rib cage.

The sun raged in a cloudless sky. At the Plaza de Toros the heat was only a few degrees below the temperature of human blood. The great bowl-shaped building brimmed with the blast-furnace afternoon. Even the section called sombra was still an hour away from shadow, and the better-paying customers sweltered along with those in the cheap seats as the trumpets called and the banda taurina began to play.

The empresario Don Pepe was in a jubilant mood. He stood sweating behind the barrera, watching the paseo with his friend Lucky Sam Wo, whose own mood was every bit as alegre. "What a crowd," Don Pepe enthused. "Not a vacant seat."

"You should see the mob outside," Lucky Sam said. "Police everywhere; ten squadrons at least. The heist men and second-story operators must be having a fiesta in town."

The procession of the toreros began. Paco Machismo and la Fabalita marched side by side, ahead of the banderilleros and picadors. The girl's head was high, her fighting-cock strut every bit the equal of Paco Machismo's arrogant swagger. She wore her long black hair tied in a single braid down her back. The crowd applauded and called out, "Hola, Paco," and "Bravo, Fabalita."

"Listen to them, they love her," Don Pepe said. "She's going to be a sensation."

"It would seem so," the Chinese inventor replied.

"How's the machine? Everything working?"

"Mototoro is ready. I checked him out myself when we got to the arena. He's running on automatic now. The handlers behind the toril gate could not believe it wasn't a live animal. My creation waits in darkness, Pepe, but when the gate is opened and sunlight hits the photoelectric cells in his glass eyes, he will come alive; more alive than any farm-bred bull ever dreamed of being."

La Fabalita fumed in the center of the arena. Scattered applause greeted her entrance but she did little to acknowledge it. Her pants were too tight and the discomfort only added to her displeasure. What should have been a triumph, the return to the bullring of Esmeralda Fabada, espontánea, under contract as la Fabalita, matador de toros, had been soured by the insulting behavior of Paco Machismo. She wasn't fooled by his exaggerated courtliness; the elaborate hand-kissing was as sharp a rebuke as a slap in the face. He thought her a foolish woman and she vowed that before the afternoon was out she would give el número uno a lesson in the art of bullfighting he would never forget.

The enthusiastic entry of Mototoro into the arena occasioned an astonished murmuring among a crowd expecting something more along the lines of a steam tractor to come clanking out of the toril gate. Fabalita's animosity dissolved the instant she unfurled the canvas cape and began her first media veronica. The machine was no ordinary bull. It was a bull such as a matador might face only two or three times each season: brave, straight-charging, reacting promptly to the swirl of the cape. Mototoro was the answer to a torero's prayers.

Fabalita worked closer and closer to the horns. Her movements had the precision and fire of poetry; sonnets and sestinas flowed from her cape; her slippered feet traced couplets and quatrains in the sand; iambic hoofbeats answered her passionate chanting: "Toro . . . toro . . . toro. . . ."

The ritual continued unaltered by the fact that Mototoro was a machine and not a bull. The picadors used blunt-tipped lances so as not to damage delicate internal mechanisms, but Mototoro was programmed to charge the silhouette of a horse without hesitation, and a number of small switches inserted in the robot's morillo simulated severed neck muscles when hit by the pica. Artificial blood flowed freely. Fabalita placed three pairs of specially designed magnetic banderillas. The crowd cheered and clapped, won over by the illusion.

The final tercio was an intricate choreography of death. La Fabalita's skill with the muleta touched on the lyrical, a perfect counterpoint to Mototoro's somber majesty. The kill was made with a single thrust, recibiendo, the sword going straight to the off button deep within Mototoro's electrical nervous system. The machine dropped to its knees and rolled slowly onto its back, gushing simulated gore.

Ten thousand hats sailed into the air in celebration. The judges awarded Fabalita both ears and the tail, but when Lucky Sam Wo saw the monosabios advancing on his invention with knives drawn, he bounded from behind the barrera and presented the triumphant matador with a duplicate set of severed bull parts bought at a butcher shop that morning in case of just such an eventuality.

Paco Machismo joined in the tumultuous applause, clapping enthusiastically as la Fabalita paraded past on her triumphal tour of the arena. "She has a lot of style, that one," he said to his manager, standing beside him behind the barrera. "I was wrong to misjudge her."

"A brilliant performance is always hard to follow, Paco," Alfredo Gazpacho said. "You must give more than your courage with the rinoceronte. Nothing but fine art will satisfy this crowd now."

"If he charges as straight as that machine, I will teach him to speak Latin before bestowing the gift of death."

"Not too close at first, Paco. Feel him out with the cape and see how he moves."

"Tell me, Alfredo, have you seen the Americans?"

"In the office, an hour ago. I spoke with the one called Abe. I asked him for the remainder of your money."

"Yes?"

"He was counting the receipts and said if I came back later he would have it ready for me."

"I don't like that. We agreed to payment on the day of the fight."

"Don't worry, Paco, the day of the fight is not over yet."

"All right, but where are the cameras? I thought this was to be a movie. How can they make a movie without cameras?"

"How should I know these things? Perhaps they have hidden the cameras. Perhaps it is *cinéma vérité*."

Paco Machismo took a long swig from the water jug, rinsed his mouth once, and spat into the dust between his feet. "I don't like this, Alfredo, something is wrong."

"What is wrong is for your mind not to be on your work. Business is my concern, killing the rhinoceros is yours. Now stop worrying about money and concentrate on what you must do, for it is time to enter the arena."

A sword-handler interrupted the self-congratulatory gloating of Don Pepe and Lucky Sam Wo to say that a lady in the first row desired to speak with the empresario. Don Pepe turned for a look. It was Arturo Madrigal's mother, Doña Carlota. She sat, somber as a bat in her

148

black dress, holding a large umbrella above her head for shade.

"Buenas tardes, Señora Madrigal," Don Pepe said, coming over and reaching up on tiptoes to kiss her pale, cold hand. "This is an unexpected pleasure."

"How long has it been since you heard such applause, Pepe?" The señora's voice was thin and weak.

"Not since Arturo. It is welcome music."

"This is your lucky day, Pepe, and for the girl too. Look how proudly Fabalita walks. They're throwing flowers. How excited she must be."

"Are you feeling ill, Señora Madrigal? You seem fatigued."

"You're very observant, Pepe," Doña Carlota said. "I'm not in the best of health, it is true. But I have taken my medicine and expect to be free of all pain and suffering very soon."

"My every wish for your speedy recovery," Don Pepe said.

"Gracias, Pepe, but your thoughts should be with la Fabalita on her day of triumph. Here she comes now; such a pretty smile. Hurry and congratulate her, Pepe, and please, give her these as a token of my admiration." Señora Madrigal reached beneath her seat and handed Don Pepe the long white box of roses. "Every young lady should have flowers to celebrate special occasions."

Don Pepe made a short bow and hurried to the barrera. A cluster of picadors and sword-handlers shook la Fabalita's hand and clapped her affectionately on the back. Lucky Sam wrapped the girl's bleeding trophies in his pocket handkerchief.

"You were magnífica, Fabalita," the empresario said, drawing the matador into an avuncular embrace. "I am honored to be your friend and associate."

149

"The machine was very brave," la Fabalita said. "I take back everything bad I said about it."

"Listen to that crowd. They love you. Today Fabalita has won two hundred thousand fans, and among them the mother of the inspired Arturo Madrigal. She asked me to give you this in appreciation."

"What is it?" Fabalita eyed the long box as she wiped the blood from her hands on a damp towel hanging behind the berrera.

"Flowers. Would you like to hold them?"

"I have no time for flowers now." La Fabalita smiled and waved to the cheering crowd. She spoke to Don Pepe from behind her frozen smile like a ventriloquist. "Have someone take them back to my hotel room, and make certain they have enough water."

"You are my queen," Don Pepe chirped foolishly, "the Empress Fabalita. Your wish is my command."

Fabalita continued to smile and wave. "Never mind the bullshit, Pepe," she said, not moving her lips, "just get those damn flowers out of here without making a speech about it."

The money was counted and stacked. Abe Wasserman wrapped each bundle with a rubber band and stuffed it into the bottom of a fat leather valise. He was starting on the last pile when Marty Farb strolled into the office, chewing a stick of gum.

"How'd it go?" Abe asked.

"Nothing to it. I left all the papers in the Chinaman's desk and destroyed his contract with us. Plus, I stuffed his wastebasket with a bunch of incriminating correspondence."

"Anybody see you going in?"

"Nah, the building was empty; most everybody in town

must be here at the bullring. How's the take?" Marty thumbed a wad of money like a dealer checking a pack of cards for marks.

"Close to seventy million pesetas."

Marty whistled. "Better'n we figured," he said.

"A lot better when you consider expenses were under a million and a half." Abe finished bundling the banknotes and snapped the suitcase shut.

"Are you leaving something in the office to finger the Chinaman?" Marty asked.

"The place is lousy with plants: dummy checks, a phony bankbook; plus, his address is printed on all the stationery. By the time the cops find that forged paper in his desk, the good professor will take the rap as the brains behind the whole operation."

"And the money?"

"They'll be checking for a yacht called the *Spoonbill*, supposedly sailing from Monaco to the Balearics."

"Perfect," Marty said, reaching for the heavy leather suitcase. "Harry's waiting at the airport. We better hustle or we'll miss our flight to Rome."

Off to one side, with his heavy cape held in both hands, Paco Machismo watched the rhino's frenzied charge across the ring. A peon provoked the attack, shaking a cape like a beach blanket and ducking back to safety behind the barrera. A shout louder than a thunderstorm greeted the fearsome beast.

When the rhinoceros turned, blinking in the bright sunlight, Paco Machismo stood alone in the center of the arena. His first pass, a media veronica, drew a loud cheer from the spectators, but Paco knew it was a sham. The rhinoceros was a myopic creature and had trouble distinguishing anything other than movement. Although it charged at full speed, executing a successful pass was no more dangerous than standing at the edge of the platform when a train roars through.

The rhinoceros skidded to a stop and Paco Machismo provoked another charge, and then a third; each pass eliciting a loud "Olé!" Linking passes together in any sort of a sequence was impossible, and Paco worried about what he would do when the time came for close work with the muleta and sword. How do you control an animal that cannot see?

The entrance of the picadors provided a distraction for Paco and a larger target for the rhino. A horse was something substantial. Draped in their quilted protective pads, they were broad as the back end of a moving van. Unlike the man with the whirling cape, the picador and his mount made no effort to avoid the impact of the berserk animal's charge. The rhinoceros lifted both padded horse and rider on the tip of his terrible horn and tossed them over the barrera into a crowd of sword-handlers and assorted peons. Before Paco rushed in to make the quite, two more picadors were down, their skinny-legged horses sprawled in the sand like a year's supply of dog food.

The rhinoceros looked up from the carnage at the matador flapping his red-and-yellow cape. Paco Machismo advanced to within ten varas of the squinting brute, shouting challenges and insults: "Run, you sow! You barrel-bellied throwback! Run!"

This was all the encouragement the rhino needed. The grunting beast drove at the man in the gold-embroidered suit, catching el número uno off balance and sending him cartwheeling into the air at the end of a four-foot horn that would be a prize addition to any Arab sheik's medicine chest.

Paco lay bleeding in the dirt and watched the rhinoceros rampage across the arena. Pain had yet to penetrate the shock of the tossing and he lay very still and considered his next move. Somehow he had to get back behind the barrera. The horn had torn into his right thigh, snapping the bone above the knee. Using his arms and elbows for traction, the matador began to drag himself, legs trailing uselessly behind, across the packed sand of the arena. Not far away, the rhinoceros detected the movement and lowered his gore-splattered head for another charge.

The moment la Fabalita saw Paco Machismo go down, she was out from behind the barrera, running across the bullring to assist him. "Cuidado, Fabalita," the crowd warned. The rhinoceros, distracted by the girl's waving cape, galloped past el número uno's prostrate form, storm clouds of dust gathering in his furious wake. Fabalita turned the two-ton animal with an elegant pass called "The Wings of an Angel," sending him crashing off to the opposite side of the arena.

"Can you walk?" she called, hurrying over to the fallen matador.

Paco Machismo lay grimacing at her feet. "I believe the bone is broken," he said. "I can't put any weight on it."

"Here, let me help you."

"No!" Paco pushed away her offered hand and pointed across the bullring. "The rinoceronte! Alerta!"

Fabalita looked up in time to see the rhinoceros bearing down full charge upon her. She stepped away from the defenseless Paco and performed a sloppy last-minute veronica as the bewildered African import roared snorting past.

"Hurry," Fabalita said, taking hold of Paco's arm. "Put

your weight on my shoulder and we can make it to the barrera."

"I don't think so," Paco Machismo said as he and la Fabalita took their first hobbling steps together. "The rinoceronte is extremely nearsighted; it charges only moving objects. When I was lying still on the ground it left me alone."

"Don't talk. Try and conserve your strength."

After driving his horn repeatedly into the toril gate, the rhinoceros backed off and looked around for something less impervious to attack. "Be on guard, Fabalita," Paco yelled, letting go of the girl's shoulder and sliding with a groan to the ground at her feet as the rhino charged. The lady matador unfurled her cape and waited, positioning herself for another veronica.

What should have been a simple maneuver was complicated by an inopportune wind flurry. The cape had not been wetted down and was suddenly unmanageable, filling with air and lifting like a sail over the rhino's head where it caught on the uplifted horn and jerked free from la Fabalita's grasp. Disarmed, the girl looked about desperately for a mono to bring another cape, but she and Paco were all alone in the arena, huddled together like survivors on a life raft as the rogue rhinoceros raged in circles around them.

Doña Carlota Madrigal sat shivering in her black dress in spite of the boiler-room heat which had thousands of spectators fanning furiously with their programs. Venom flowed through her veins like a river of ice. She felt the frozen tendrils encircling her heart. Her eyesight clouded and lengthening shadows spread across her field of vision. She knew darkness would soon engulf her.

Although the cold mists of death had gathered, the

señora was smiling and jubilant. In the darkening arena before her, la Fabalita was at the mercy of a wild rinoceronte. A fitting end for such filth: to die in this mockery of the profession to which her Arturo had brought so much glory. And even if by chance the gypsy puta survived, the roses with their fatal sting awaited her. Carlota Madrigal closed her eyes and accepted the rarest pleasure life can offer: a happy death.

Behind the barrera, two bullfight managers fussed and fluttered like distraught hens at the prospect of being rendered clientless. Alfredo Gazpacho cursed a cowering banderillero. "Get out there, hombre, and make the quite," he screamed. "You signed a contract to be in Paco's caudrilla, now get out there and do your duty or I'll see that you never work in the corrida again."

"You go out if you're so brave," the ashen-faced torero said, handing the manager his cape. "I don't care if I drive a bus for the rest of my life."

"To face that monster is suicide," piped a trembling monosabio.

"Cowards, all of you!" Gazpacho aimed a final kick at the banderillero's backside. "You're not fit to wear the suit of lights, you cheap bag of tripe."

Not far away, the empresario Don Pepe paced up and down moaning, "Oh, Fabalita . . . oh, my future, my fortune . . . oh, my poor, poor Fabalita. . . ." He wrung his hands like a housefly preening. Deep in his safe-deposit soul Don Pepe was emotionally bankrupt, but any businessman would appreciate what he was going through at the moment.

"Get down, get down," Paco Machismo demanded, hauling on la Fabalita's tasseled pant leg. "Lie down flat; hurry, so he won't see you."

"But I can't give up and hide in the sand," the girl protested.

"It is the only way. What can you do without your cape?"

Somewhat reluctantly, Fabalita knelt beside Paco. "This is wrong," she said. "I belong on my feet."

Paco grabbed her jacket with both hands and pulled her down on top of him. "Why die for nothing? Now lie still next to me and pretend to be dead. Look—see that horse twitching? The rinoceronte will see it and attack. There, what did I say? Three . . . four . . . five times he hits it with the horn."

"I pity the poor picador."

"He is safe," Paco said. "He is under the horse."

"You were a fool even to take this contract," Fabalita said. "There is no controlling that animal."

"I was drunk with the thought of so much money— borracho con dinero. It stole my senses away. But you took the same risks for nothing, Fabalita."

"I acted only to save your life, do you place no value on that?"

"There is nothing I value more," Paco said. "That is why my debt to you is beyond measure. Fabalita, listen, should that rinoceronte come our way again, I want you to get beneath me."

"What? *Never!*"

"Yes, I insist. I owe you my life. My body will protect yours from the horn thrusts."

"Paco, no—

"Fabalita, I have never seen a woman like you. You excite me more than language can describe. Let this be my way of making love to you. What better place to die could a man wish for than on top of a beautiful woman?"

"Paco . . ."

Paco lifted on his elbows and covered the upper half of her body with his. "Fabalita, mi amor," he whispered. "Mi corazón. . . ."

At first, she tried to push him away, but her hands slipped from against his chest and circled slowly up around his neck. Fabalita closed her dark eyes. As their lips met, the sound of galloping hoofbeats grew louder through the reverberating sand.

Not many blocks from the bullring, two strong-arm stick-up specialists were having a business conference and had to raise their voices above the wild uproar of the crowd. "I don't know why I keep working with you," the first thug shouted. "It's a waste of time to snatch anything you can't get rid of in a hurry."

"You said the same thing the time we grabbed that suitcase full of radio cosas and made fifteen hundred pesetas in less than half an hour."

"That was different; you can't take flowers to a fence."

"Who said anything about a fence? With roses like these you have no difficulty finding customers. Those two ricos waiting for a taxi across the street are what we want. Gentlemen who appreciate quality."

"We ought to grab that suitcase is what we ought to do. It looks like real pigskin."

"Too many people around. One thing at a time, amigo, now watch this. —Hola, señores, I could not help noticing that you are about to embark on a voyage, perhaps—"

"Sorry, buddy, no hoblay Español."

"Oh, you Americano?"

"That's right."

"Okay, no problem, I spik good engliss. You go now onna treep, yes?"

"Heading straight to the airport, pal. You got a great

little country here and don't let anybody ever tell you different."

"Berry good. Maybe you like buy something nice for the lobbed juans at home, yes?"

"What's he selling, Abe?"

"I don't know. Whatcha got, buddy?"

"Rosas. Mira: berry preety, yes?"

"Not bad."

"You name for President Abe Leancone, yes?"

"How much?"

"Dígame?"

"How much for the flowers?"

"Only five hundred pesetas, senor. Berry chip, yes?"

"I'll give you three fifty, not a penny more."

"Tree hunner an feefty? Okay, cómo no? We make a deal, yes?"

"Sure, buddy, it's a deal, Pay the man, Marty, all I got is traveler's checks. Lulu loves flowers, she'll just die when she gets these."

Each time the rhinoceros drove his lancelike horn into the belly of the dead horse, the outcry from the crowd grew louder until it seemed the human voice was incapable of such a sound. But when Paco Machismo, trailing blood across the sand, pulled the lovely Fabalita into a passionate embrace before the astonished eyes of two hundred thousand fans, the wail of outrage and pain which arose was something altogether inhuman.

Lucky Sam Wo spoke in a whisper in spite of the din. Paco Machismo's manager had to bend down to within a centimeter of his lips in order to hear: "Will you guarantee expenses?"

"Guarantee what?" Gazpacho demanded.

"Only Mototoro can save them now," the Chinese inventor said, "but I must look after my own investment as well."

"The machine, of course, why didn't I think of it? I'll pay anything it's worth, but hurry, Paco's hurt, this may be his last chance."

Lucky Sam reached into his pocket for the control unit and pressed a sequence of buttons. An instant later, the heavy wooden planks of the toril gate disintegrated as if they were no more than a paper hoop and Mototoro rumbled into the arena like the Red Ball Express. The sound of his entrance was lost in the general tempest. Unalarmed, the rhinoceros poked and prodded among the bunched intestines of a dead horse.

Charging with Euclidian precision, Mototoro streaked across the diameter of the bullring. At the last minute, the rhinoceros raised his head, standing his ground as the determined machine drove headlong into his midsection. Grunting and squealing, the big animal dropped to his knees, scrambling free as the robot slashed and stabbed.

Mototoro circled to one side as the rhinoceros got back on his feet, bleeding copiously from the wounds in his flank. Although badly hurt, the African giant still outweighed his mechanical adversary by several hundred kilos. This statistic was not lost on Mototoro, and the four-legged data processor kept a wary camera lens focused on the lumbering rhino. At a point midway between the two circling combatants, la Fabalita and Paco Machismo lay French-kissing in the sand, oblivious to their predicament and the insane screaming of the crowd.

The rhinoceros initiated the attack, stumbling forward and feinting with his large horn, until Mototoro moved in for the kill. But the wily rhino anticipated the first thrust, parrying like a swordsman and sidestepping with unexpected agility. The robot was thrown off balance, skidding awkwardly in a confused effort to get away as the rhinoceros hammered against his sheet-metal bodywork. Again and again the four-foot horn found its mark with a gong-like resonance.

Behind the barrera, the bullfight managers were frantic. "The machine is finished. They're doomed," Alfredo Gazpacho wailed. Lucky Sam Wo continued to smile as he tapped out new instructions on his pocket-sized control unit. Out in the arena, the entwined figures of the fallen matadors were lost in the swirling dust.

When the haze settled, a dented Mototoro and a bleeding rhinoceros stood at opposite sides of the bullring. Mammal and machine looked one another in the eye for a moment long enough to suggest real communication, and, as if on signal, they lowered their weaponry like knights at a tournament and began to charge. They met head to head at the center of the arena with the sound of a dozen television sets falling down the stairs. A bright blue ball of electrical fire preceded the actual explosion. Mototoro went off in a burst of space-age pyrotechnics, spraying rhinoburger and spare parts high into the air.

As the cloud of white smoke lifted, a patch of scorched sand was revealed, along with what little remained to mark the fight of the century: a stray hoof, assorted cogs, oddments of raw meat. Not far from the carnage, Paco Machismo and la Fabalita remained locked in each other's arms. Neither the robust entrance of the robot nor the subsequent holocaust had disturbed their embrace. Fabalita was reaching into Paco's gold-embroidered trousers when the men with the stretchers came running up. The photographers were close behind. Life was never the same again for either of them.